Carlo Gébler
Frozen Out
A TALE OF BETRAYAL AND SURVIVAL

mammoth

The author gratefully acknowledges the financial support of the Arts Council/
An Chomhairle Ealaíon while writing this book

First published in Great Britain 1998
by Mammoth, an imprint of Reed International Books Limited
Michelin House, 81 Fulham Road, London SW3 6RB

ISBN 0 7497 2874 4

10 9 8 7 6 5 4 3 2 1

A CIP catalogue record for this title is available from the British Library

Typeset by Avon Dataset Ltd, Bidford on Avon, Warwickshire
Printed in Great Britain by Cox & Wyman Ltd, Reading, Berkshire

Contents

PART THREE
Frozen Out

Seeing's believing, but *feeling* is God's own truth.

Ulster Proverb

For my friends,
Jason and Victoria Hartcup

Author's Note

Co. Fermanagh and the town of Enniskillen are real places. However, neither the village of Crookedstone, nor the Farmer's Memorial Primary School, the Enniskillen Girl's Academy, or Our Lady of Fatima Grammar School, are to be found on any maps. That is because they are invented, as are all the characters and situations described in this novel.

PART ONE
Coming to Fermanagh

1 The day before we left

I woke up on July 11th 1992, with that strange feeling I get when something's not right but I can't exactly remember what it is.

I lay there and looked at the ceiling. It was white and bumpy, cracks here and there. Dad put his foot through the corner when he was in the loft and he patched it himself with Polyfilla. I could see the face of a dragon up there.

I still couldn't remember what was up, so I did what I always do.

When we were on holiday in Italy I lost my passport, and ever since, in case it ever happens again, I've made certain I've got all the facts off by heart; Passport number, 009817174. Surname, Rodgers, given name, Phoebe. British citizen, born 3rd September, 1981, London. Sex, female. Number of children, none.

I am ten. I have brown eyes and black hair. I have no interesting moles or distinguishing scars. I am the daughter of David and Kate Rodgers. I have two

3

brothers – Fred who is four and Tom who is seven. I live at 165, Acacia Road, North Kensington, London W10 7TY.

Something banged downstairs, and I remembered.

I had begun my last day at 165 Acacia Road. Tomorrow I'd be waking somewhere else, and the day after tomorrow I'd be waking in my new bedroom, at the Glebe House, Tully something or other, in Ireland.

Inside me I felt like I had goose bumps. I realised I had better get up, and say goodbye to what I knew.

Downstairs, the pictures were stacked by the front door, and beside them were a bank of cardboard boxes filled with Dad's books.

When ever I go past anything with writing on it, I read, so I read the writing on the boxes: *Conference Pears Special Fruit, Covial French Apples, Sainsbury's Milk Chocolate Digestives.* The hall smelt of coffee and Play Doh, which is like marzipan, and the polish Mum puts on the wooden floor, and on top of these there was the smell of bacon.

In the kitchen Mum was peering under the grill, and Hector, our cat, was peering up at Mum. He's very partial to bacon.

'I thought we'd have a treat,' said Mum, and then she stared at me, and squinted. 'Did you sleep well?

You look tired, Phoebe. You've got black rings under your eyes.'

It was true. Using the Playskool torch Tom got for Christmas, I'd stayed up reading *The Lion, the Witch and the Wardrobe* by C.S. Lewis, because at the back of the book it said the writer came from Belfast, the capital of Northern Ireland. It didn't say anything about where we were going, but I loved it and read three chapters. I didn't tell Mum this.

I heard the television in the front room and went through. It was 'The Big Breakfast'. Dad always objects when he's in the house, but luckily he was out. He says 'The Big Breakfast' is visual chewing gum and rubbish, and an indictment of falling standards. He's a journalist. 'Bad television is a Trojan horse.' That's another favourite of his. We all go, 'Yeah, Dad,' when he says this, but none of us have a clue what he's on about. He tries to be strict but more often than not he can't carry it off. I don't think he's always got his feet on the ground, but he's still lovely.

Mum called, 'Come and get it,' and I raced Tom and Fred to the kitchen table. She'd put the bacon on bread with melted butter and blackcurrant jam, our usual Sunday morning treat.

'It's a moving treat,' she said.

'Mum, you know in the back of my passport in the page marked Emergencies?'

'Yes.'

'We're going to have to change the address to the Glebe, Tully whatever it is.'

'Yes,' she agreed absent-mindedly.

'Otherwise, if I get sick or something, they'll send me here and it wouldn't be my home any more.'

'But, Phoebe, we're not going abroad. You don't need a passport to go to Ireland, whether you go to the north or the south.'

'Why not?' asked Tom.

'I'm not quite certain,' said Mum, 'I'll have to ask Dad.'

'What's the address anyhow?' I asked.

'The Glebe House, Tullyloman, Crookedstone, Co. Fermanagh, Northern Ireland, BT74 6YT,' said Mum, and then she added, 'Impressed I know the post code?'

Nodding, I repeated BT74 6YT a few times to myself and took a bite of my bacon sarnie. I chewed on the right side because I've got a gap on the upper left side and it's horrible when bacon gets caught in there.

The doorbell rang and four removal men marched into our house wearing brown coats. Suddenly the kitchen was empty except for the table and the chairs we were sitting on.

''Fraid I'm going to need them, love,' said one of the removal men. Hector was on the table, waiting for a bacon rind I held pinched between my fingers.

'Get down,' said Mum, and pushed Hector off. He ran to the corner where his basket stood before it was whisked away, and he began to miaow.

Everything that had always been around me and familiar had been whipped away in a matter of minutes. I felt a sort of kick and I saw the removal man looking at me, turning the ring on his finger, and I thought, oh no, I'm going to cry. I must not do that.

Mum saw, of course. Sometimes I think she can see right inside my head.

'Why don't you run round to see Sylvia?' Mum said in her gentle voice, the coaxing one. I don't get it much nowadays; she reserves it mainly for the boys, mostly for Fred, who's impossible because he thinks he's the baby even if he is four years old, so I liked hearing it now.

'Yes.'

'What if my toys get left behind?' said Fred, tears in his eyes and his lower lip quivering. 'You haven't put them in a box!' he cried. That's typical of the little brat. In point of fact (I got that phrase from Dad – it's a good one, isn't it?) he had refused to let Mum box anything up – and now, here he was, complaining they weren't in a box.

'Goodbye,' I said, and I got up and ran from the house.

Sylvia lives in the corner house at the end of the street.

I found her in her bedroom playing with her Sylvanian figures.

'They're putting all our furniture in the pantechnicon,' I said proudly.

Sylvia gathered her blonde hair at the back and pulled it round to the front. She sniffed.

'I think the Sylvanians are due a move too, don't you?' she said.

'We'd need a pantechnicon.'

'We'll use my brother's Playmobil ambulance,' she said.

'Where are the Sylvanians going?' she asked, more of herself than of me, and I thought, where am I going? Dad had said there were bats living in the Glebe House, and probably mice, but he promised they'd all be gone by the time we moved in.

'Do you think it'll be nice in Ireland?'

'I don't know.'

'I could come and visit.'

'You must.'

I put the bats out of my thoughts and imagined standing outside the yellow front of the house and Sylvia standing beside me. That's the mind for you; one moment you're sad, the next you're worried about something, and the third you're happy because of something that might not even happen.

'You know, I really think I will come,' said Sylvia.

'I hope so.'

'You know,' she said, 'I really think it's time for me to be independent, to stand on my own two feet. I really think I should start to branch away from my family.'

I was happy when I ran into the house.

'Is that you?' shouted Mum from the kitchen.

'Yeah,' I said, and tore upstairs and into my bedroom. Almost everything was gone.

All day I'd had this feeling on and off, of a big bag inside me and it was filling up with water and now I knew the time had come for it to burst and I was going to cry.

I let out a great wail and went and lay down on the futon in the corner. It was hard, not like lying on my old bed. I wanted something softer. I put my head on the pillow, and smelt the lovely musty smell of *The Lion, the Witch and the Wardrobe* which Mum had left there for me, and then gave myself over to the hurt inside that was as real as a bruise or a cut only you couldn't see it, and a great hot salty tear came out of my eye and went over my cheek and into my mouth.

A few minutes later Mum came into the room. She closed the door softly after herself and looked at me for a moment or two, then came over, gathered her skirt around her legs and sat down on the futon and swept

9

my hair back and wiped my eyes with the end of her cuff. I liked that. It was just her and me again, just like before the boys came.

'Listen, pet, it's a wrench, leaving here, home, friends, and all that, but it's where he comes from, your dad, and he wants to go back. There's a job, a good job with a local paper. I won't have to go out to work. I can stay at home with the boys for a while. We've got a good price for this house, and the house we're buying in Northern Ireland is bigger than this and will cost far less than anything we'd buy here . . .'

Then she stopped talking and shook her head like she does when she knows she's started down the wrong track and wants to say something different.

'What am I saying? What am I saying? We go on and on, we Mums and Dads, talking as if our children understand every word. Look, it's very frightening ripping out our roots here and transplanting the family to this faraway, strange place – well, not that faraway, we have been there for holidays, but it certainly isn't London, is it?

'Look,' Mum continued, 'if it doesn't work, we'll come back, but honestly, pet, we wouldn't be doing it if we didn't think it was the right thing to do.'

She held me then. Hard and tight, like I was baby.

I drifted away. I was not asleep but I was not awake either. Where her cheek touched mine the skin was roasting. When she stirred, I felt a bit like I was coming out of a dream, and when I blinked my eyes I felt my sad feeling had gone.

In the evening Dad said we'd all been under a lot of stress and it was time for a treat. We had a take-away hamburger and we ate with our hands, sitting in a circle on the floor.

'Just like a Red Indian feast,' said Fred, who was wearing his feathered head-dress and his buckskin jacket with his Sheriff's badge pinned on the breast. I had a double hamburger with cheese, mild pickle, fried onions and mayonnaise on a sesame bun, large chips, and large root beer. Afterwards, Dad produced a half-gallon tub of honeycomb ice-cream and told us we had to eat every morsel because we had no freezer for leftovers. It was a struggle but we managed.

'I'll miss this old house,' said Dad, with Hector drowsing on his lap.

'I don't think we want to talk about that,' said Mum. 'Phoebe,' she said, 'would you go and get your glass animals?'

I stood up and I thought I was going to fall over. I'd never felt so full.

'Can't. I'm stuffed.'

'Go on. They're in the bath. Bring them down, please.'

I've got more than fifty glass animals which I've collected over the years. They're my passion. Among other things I have two zebras, a lion, a lioness, an African elephant, five penguins of diminishing size, a scarlet macaw, a koala bear, a giant green tree frog, a salt water crocodile, and a platypus. The time I lost my passport I was in a glass blowing factory near Venice and my passport was in the glove compartment of our car in the car park. The car was stolen and the passport went with it. Dad was furious. But I'll always remember that day, because, at the end of the tour I was presented with a clear glass dolphin, with a blue spine, leaping through the air, and he is probably my favourite.

Much later, when I was lying on the futon, I heard Mum and Dad in the front garden under my window, ferrying the last boxes out to the car. They were in high spirits, excited and giddy, like they only get at Christmas or when they drink together. They made so much noise, old Mrs Lynch from across the road shouted, 'Bit of quiet, please.'

It *was* quiet downstairs after that, and as I lay there waiting for sleep, listening to the lorries on Scrubs Lane, the trains shunting on the goods line on the other side of Little Wormwood Scrubs, I looked up at the ceiling. I could see my dragon and I began to wonder who would lie here and look up at him when we were gone.

2 Our journey

Mum woke me very early. I was in a trance but I got dressed somehow and got into the car and went straight back to sleep. A few moments later she woke me again as she bundled my futon and the sleeping bag into the back.

'Have you forgotten anything?' she said.

As I thought about her question, I could hear Hector. He was in his travelling box in the back, running a claw up and down one of the bumpy walls inside.

'Is there any reason you need to go back inside?' she said.

I looked at the house and huge magnolia bush that grows at the front. I shook my head.

'Certain?'

'I think so.'

'We're going to post the keys through the letter-box.'

'OK.'

'Tom? Fred? Have you left anything behind? Have you both done a wee?'

'Yes,' the boys groaned.

'All right,' she called to Dad, who was standing at the front door.

'OK,' he shouted back. He lifted the small brass flap of the letter-box and posted the keys through.

Then he walked slowly down the path and out the gate. He closed the gate very carefully after himself and turned. He looked at the 'Sold' sign and then at the house. He stayed there quite a long time. Then he came and got into the driving seat beside Mum, turned the key in the ignition, and drove slowly away.

Dad didn't say anything and Mum was quiet as well. His hand was on the gear stick and I saw her squeeze his hand as it rested there. Then Mum pinched on either side of her nose a couple of times, which she does when she doesn't want to cry.

I turned and looked through the window at London gliding by.

After that we drove for hours and hours and hours on the motorway, and we didn't stop until the evening, when we reached a hotel near Stranraer. We were allowed to bring Hector in with us into the family room we got. There was a little fridge in the corner and Dad's eyes lit up when he saw it. 'I think I need a drink,' he said.

Dad turned the key in the little lock but the door wouldn't open. He began to pull on the handle.

'Don't force it,' Mum advised but he wouldn't listen.

He put his feet on the door, grasped the handle and pulled back with all his might.

The handle came away with a horrible screech and Dad flew back and hit his head on the corner of one of the beds.

I felt I might laugh but I knew it was better not to. I picked up Hector and began to stroke him behind the ears and he immediately started to purr.

'You know what's wrong with modern life?' shouted Dad, rubbing the side of his head. 'It's all gone to pot. Everything's plastic nowadays.'

After breakfast the next morning, we drove to the harbour to catch the ferry to Northern Ireland. A policeman came and asked us if we'd packed the car ourselves, and then we had to open the back and show him all our luggage and Hector's travelling box, and he asked Dad again if we had packed the car ourselves.

I said, 'We don't have any bombs,' and Mum said, 'Shut up.'

Then we had to queue for a long time, and finally a man in a peaked hat and bright yellow coat waved us forward.

We got on to the car deck and I got out. It smelt of diesel and oil. The metal floor was slimy and oily. And I could hear men shouting and screaming.

At first I couldn't quite hear what they were saying.

But as my ears got used to the place, I could understand perfectly:

'Away with the Pope and the IRA,
All the way with the UDA.'

Dad came up to me. He'd heard. He looked grim. I could see Fred holding on to Dad's hand really tightly. And I saw Mum's face, too. She was nervous.

'It's just high spirits,' said Dad, in the voice he used when he was making light of something.

Mum swallowed and wiped her face with her hand.

A coach pulled up beside us. Men started to file down the stairs. They were all shouting and laughing and carrying on, just the same as the men I'd heard shouting earlier. Some of them were carrying drums and flutes, while others had their arms filled with cases of beer.

'Don't gawp at the Orangemen,' I heard Dad saying beside me, and at that moment a man came up, middle-aged, and with a bit of a tummy. Security, according to his peaked cap.

'Their bark's worse than their bite,' he said. A pair of very shiny handcuffs dangled from his belt. 'But I'd keep on the safe side of them all the same,' he said.

Another coach drew up, flags in the windows, and a huge banner in the back showing a man on a white horse and the words *Remember 1690* underneath.

This was William of Orange. And I knew what all this was about, as well. Dad had explained it to me. A long time ago, France and Spain were Catholic, but England was Protestant. There was a lot of bad feeling between the countries because of religion. James II was the King of England and Ireland at the time. Some people said he was a Catholic, others that his wife was. But William, a relative of James (although I don't remember the connection exactly), was a Protestant, and many people wanted him to be King instead of James.

William of Orange came to Ireland and there were many big battles. The biggest was at the Boyne. This was in 1690. James II was defeated at this battle and afterwards William became King, King William III. Ever since then, all over Northern Ireland, men who are called Orangemen march on the 12th July to celebrate this victory. And Orangemen come from other places to march with them. A lot of them come from Scotland. That's who all these people were. They were Scottish Orangemen who were on their way to march the next day, which was the 12th July.

The door of the coach with the banner slid open and another load of rowdy men got out. It was scary, the way they just kept coming. These ones carried drums and bagpipes, and some of them wore kilts.

'If I was you,' said the security guard, 'I'd go to the Motorists' Lounge. Follow the stairs all the way to the top, go across the deck and you have it. Go in there, close the door, and don't come out until we get to Larne.'

'I can't believe it,' said Dad, as we struggled up the stairs. 'I come from here. I should have known. Don't travel the day before the Twelfth marches. I must be insane! How could I have forgotten?'

'Darling,' said Mum, 'it's going to be all right. We're just going to sit tight in the Motorists' Lounge. The Orangemen will want to be out on the deck in the sun. They won't bother us.'

'I hope so,' he said.

'I'm sure they'll stay outside. If you were them, wouldn't you?'

We reached the Motorists' Lounge. A big hand-written notice was stuck behind the glass door:

This lounge is for divers. It is not for bandsmen.

'Why can nobody spell any more?' said Dad grimly. He opened the door and we all ran in. It was a big room filled with tables and sunlight.

'Does the door lock?' Mum wondered.

A load of men were jostling at the top of the stairs behind us. They had shaken up their beer cans and were squirting the beer from inside at each other. Dad shut the door and the sound from outside mostly disappeared.

'Wouldn't that be wonderful if it locked!' Dad twisted the handle to see if it did.

'Yes, wouldn't it just!' said the man at the table nearest the door. He was quite old, he was bald, and the top of his head was brown and shiny. His wife was with him and she was holding his hand tightly.

'I understand they have to travel,' said the bald man, 'but why must they make such a racket? And why must they strut around like they own the place?'

'It's the Orangemen's day of liberty,' said Dad, and then he added, 'Why did I choose July 11th to travel?'

'My sentiments entirely,' said the bald man. 'But I tell you, I'm glad to see you. I thought it was just going to be us and them.'

He jerked a finger towards the deck. On the other side of the glass door a group of men in blue uniforms with gold buttons were playing football. They all had little hats which were tucked under the gold braid on their shoulders.

Then their football went overboard and a great cry of 'Wa – lly, wa – lly,' went up. They all ran to the side of the boat and peered down at the sea. I nudged Dad and he smiled at the row of blue backs.

'Football on a boat. Never a good idea,' said Dad.

We sat. I got out my book of crossword puzzles but it was hard to concentrate. There was a bagpipe droning somewhere and a drum keeping time with it. On top of that, every couple of minutes it seemed, Orangemen would see us through the window and bang on the glass to get our attention, and when we looked up, they would give us the 'thumbs-up' sign, or toast us with their cans of Tennent's beer, or shout, 'Come on, come out in the sun.' It was like being an animal in the zoo.

After a while I felt the boat juddering and Dad said, 'We're off.'

I was trying to solve the clue 'Boy's name which is part of a fruit?' when I heard the door banging open and peels of laughter, and a high-pitched voice shouting, 'Get in there, Jimmy.'

I looked up and saw about twenty Orangemen were just through the door.

'This is the Motorists' Lounge,' said the bald man. 'This is for us because we've come in motor cars. It is not for you because *you* have come in coaches.'

'No, it's not, it's for divers!' squawked someone I couldn't see, and the handwritten sign, that had been stuck up on the door, flew across the room as a paper ball and hit the far wall.

'Move on,' shouted someone outside, and the ones at the front lurched forward, and dozens and dozens and dozens of men pushed into the room.

'These seats taken?' asked a man with two black eyes and a cardboard box under his arm. He wore a blue uniform.

'Help yourself,' said my dad, and about twelve more in the same blue uniform sat down around us. I pretended to look at my book while really looking around the room. There were Orangemen at every table, on the floor, on all the window ledges, blowing into their flutes, banging their drums, drinking from their cans of beer.

I reached out and found Dad's hand on the seat beside me. He squeezed my fingers. I wanted to get up and run out but I was not certain my legs could carry me. I could see more of them outside through the window beside us, lying in the sun without their T-shirts, very pale and white, but with muscles under the skin and on their arms tattoos of flags, bulldogs, and the man on the horse and *Remember 1690* underneath.

Then, suddenly, everything stopped, and I didn't like it at all. I read over the clue again in the crossword book. 'Boy's name which is part of a fruit.' Hopeless.

Then I heard a voice saying, 'Can't you read?'

I didn't want to but I looked up.

'Can't you read?' repeated the bald-headed man. 'It says "No Smoking".'

He got up and walked across the room to a man in a blue track-suit puffing on a cigarette.

'Jock, it says "No Smoking".'

The smoker took a big puff on his cigarette and blew the smoke out. You could hear a pin drop.

But then, ever so, ever so slowly, the man in the blue track-suit lifted his cigarette over to the Harp can he had in his other hand, then he dropped the cigarette through the hole and there was a sizzle sound inside as the cigarette plopped into the beer.

The man with the bald head walked back to his table. Someone said something and then someone else said something, and there were a few notes from a flute, and there was a hiss or two as a ring pull came off, and then everything was all right again.

Anyway, after that, the bandsman with the black eyes took crisps and sandwiches and bars of chocolate out of the cardboard box. He handed food around to his friends and then he offered me a sandwich and Mum said it was OK to take it and I did. He talked to Dad about the town in Scotland where he came from and the lack of work. He told Dad his name was Len and he and Dad shook hands.

Then Len said to me, 'What you doing?'

'Crossword,' I said. I was really listening to him and Dad talking.

'Yes, but what's the clue?'

' "Boy's name which is part of a fruit?" '

'Oh, that's easy.'

'I can't get it.'

'It's "Pip", isn't it?'

'Oh, yeah.'

'Do you want some crisps? You and your brothers?'

I looked at Mum and she nodded.

'Where you headed?' said Len as we ate the crisps he gave us.

'We're going to Crookedstone,' I said.

'Oh yeah, that's down there in Fermanagh, isn't it?'

'We're going to live there,' I said, and then I felt Dad prodding me in the leg.

'We might see you at the march then?' said Len. 'That's where we're marching.'

'Oh yes,' said Dad, in the voice he uses when he doesn't mean something. 'We may stay in Belfast, it depends.'

'Oh,' said the Orangeman, sounding a bit disappointed, and then he looked at me and he said, 'Would you like a *Club Orange*?'

'Oh, yes please.'

'They're good, aren't they?' said Len, 'the *Orange* biscuit,' and he winked at me broadly.

3 We arrive

We drove off the ferry and into Larne. There were flags everywhere and big arches across the road, and pictures of William of Orange on his horse and Queen Elizabeth, like on the stamps.

The countryside outside the town was green and hilly, with little houses and farms scattered here and there. The sun was shining very hard, and sometimes it reflected back from the corrugated roofs of the farm buildings and I had to blink it was so bright.

I fell asleep and woke up. The boys were hot and grumpy. Mum bought us all an ice-cream in a village, a Mr Whippy, with a chocolate stick and hundreds and thousands.

'When I was a child we called that a poke,' said Dad as we licked our ice-creams, 'and we got one, only one, on the same day each year, when we went to Portrush for our one-day annual trip to the seaside.'

'And I lived in a house with tiny windows and a leaking thatched roof,' laughed Mum and then she pretended to play a violin and went 'Wah-wah-wah-wah,' like she was playing a sad tune.

'We had a slate roof,' said Dad, and then he added, 'How will I trust you again when all you do is mock?'

'Only joking,' said Mum, and she took her lipstick out and began to put it on.

I saw Glebe House from the main road. It's a big square house, painted yellow, with black gutters and drainpipes. It has four little gable windows in the roof, and three first floor windows, and two ground floor windows, and a big, big door between them, black with a brass knocker in the middle and a fan light above, just like the house a child would draw.

We turned on to the lane, the boys shouting, 'Yippee, we're here.' The lane was dust and the dust was yellow as well, but not as yellow as the house, and it ran along beside a small river, or a big stream, depending on your point of view, and the stream was filled with cold, clear, clean water, and big rocks that were brown and black.

At the end there was a bridge and the bridge took us over the stream to the house on the other side. It was a stone bridge with an arch underneath and just when we reached the hump in the middle of the bridge, I was able to see past the house, and the turf shed and the byre at the back with their corrugated roofs, to the small lake into which the stream fed, and the small lake was like a little silver mirror, with rushes growing around it that were like a little ruff of lace.

But the glimpse only lasted a second, because then we were off the hump and down and on to the ground on the far side of the stream, and the little lake was hidden by the house in front of us, and we had arrived.

We got out and stretched, and the boys ran around screeching. I looked at the house, and I saw all the shutters were closed up behind the windows inside, and because they were painted white, I imagined they were the white eyelids of a sleeping giant.

Dad produced a big knobbly black key, opened the front door and went inside and opened each shutter, then each window, and when he had finished he came out and shouted, 'OK, it's safe. You can come in,' with a great smile on his face. The giant was awake, still a little drowsy, but friendly.

Everyone ran in. I felt very funny then. I had a smile on one side of my face and a tear on the other. Dad came over.

'Come on. Come in. This is the start of our new life.'

'I miss our old house,' I said.

'I miss our old house but this is our new house.'

He guided me in through the door.

Dad was in the study, speaking on the telephone to the removals firm, and Mum was in the doorway, leaning against the lintel and biting her lip, and Hector was on the floor looking up at her.

'So when is our furniture going to get here?' asked Dad crossly, and then he exploded.

'Tomorrow! Are you telling me that the pots and pans we need to cook with tonight, the tables and chairs we need to sit on tonight, the beds we need to sleep on tonight, will not be here until tomorrow?'

There was a long pause and then Dad put down the phone.

'Well,' said Mum, 'I suppose we'll just have to improvise.'

I helped Mum and Dad to unpack the back of the car and carry everything into the house. I didn't see my box of glass animals. I ran back to the car.

'Dad,' I said, 'my glass animals aren't in the house.'

I knew I'd lost them, but at the same time I was hoping and praying he would say he had got them. I can always go on hoping even when I know it's hopeless.

'Really?' said Dad, and then he called to Mum, 'Where's the box of Phoebe's glass animals?' She was over by the flower-bed pulling up weeds to get rid of her anger because we had no furniture.

'Isn't it in the car?' Mum called back. She pulled out something green and very ugly. She sounded casual, as if she didn't care that these were my most precious things.

'No.'

'Do you remember putting it in the car last night?'

'I can't because I only carried everything from the house,' said Dad firmly, 'and your job was to pack the car because that's your department.

'It must have fallen off the wall and into the magnolia bush behind, and in the darkness I didn't notice. Oh Phoebe, I'm so sorry!'

I felt as if a bucket of cold water had been emptied on to my head.

'Oh Phoebe, I'm so sorry,' said Mum, and she wrapped her arms around me, and pulled my head against her chest. I stayed quite still, didn't wail or sob, didn't lift my arms and clutch around her middle, just stood as I was and imagined the box.

'I'll ring Mr Harkins,' said Dad. This was the new owner.

Dad came back a few minutes later, rubbing and clapping his hands, trying to be jolly.

'Good news. The Harkins have the box, safe and sound.'

'I'm going to ring Sylvia's mum,' I said, 'and see if she'll post them.'

'Good thinking, Batman,' said Mum, and she kissed me on the forehead as I walked past her on the way to the house.

Because I was upset, Dad asked me on the blanket

foraging expedition, and not the boys. We drove to the next farm and got out. I looked through a barn door and saw a couple of cows scratching their heads on a rail. In a corner of the yard there were vast parcels of black plastic that were as tall as me and had weird white lines painted all over them (these were silage bundles Dad told me and the lines were to keep the birds off), while in another corner there was a black and white sheepdog tied with blue twine to a ring in the wall. The dog was asleep but he quickly woke up when we appeared and ran forward, as far as the string would let him, and began to bark at us, viciously. There was no one around, but it was like being in a film and I was sure we were being watched.

'Hello,' called Dad, 'anyone at home?' but all we heard were the cows as they scratched and the dog as it barked. Dad took my hand.

There was a brick bungalow and we went to the front door and knocked, and after a long time an old woman came and opened the door. She was bent, with grey hairs growing out of her chin, and the brightest, shiniest blue eyes I've ever seen.

'There's nobody here, now go away,' she said so angrily that I felt my whole stomach shrivel to the size of a walnut and lift up into my throat.

Dad gave his name and began to explain who we were and that we were stuck because our furniture lorry

29

had broken down in Wales. 'Would it be possible to borrow some blankets?' he asked. 'We'd be so grateful.'

'There's nobody here,' she screamed back at him. 'Now go away!'

I was really scared of her so we drove away quickly. We went to a shop at a crossroads in the middle of the country with a fireplace in the corner, and a coal fire burning in the grate. I liked that. Then we went home and Dad lit our fire in the front room, and we fried eggs and bread in a heavy black frying pan Mum had found in the scullery.

I went to bed in the back of the car where my brothers were already asleep under the car blankets Dad had managed to buy in the shop. I could smell the turf burning in the fireplace in our front room. I could hear Mum and Dad talking by the door. I could hear the water in the stream running over the stones along the bed, gushing and gurgling and tinkling. It was getting dark but it wasn't quite night and through the window I saw a bat jerking across the sky. I hoped it hadn't come from inside our house.

Then Mum and Dad stopped talking, and that was when I noticed how quiet it was. In London, I always found the noises outside comforting while I lay there waiting to fall asleep, because they reminded me that people were going about their lives.

It was going to be so different here – only us and

the stream – and I wondered whether, if I concentrated very hard, I could hear the sound of the grass growing, or the leaves on the trees breathing, or the feet of the little animals in the fields, scuffing the ground as they moved around?

I held my breath and tried to hear, and that was it, I fell asleep.

4 The first morning

The next morning there was no sign of the pantechnicon, so Dad took us to Crookedstone to see the parade. It mainly consisted of a lot of men in bowler hats, all carrying banners of William of Orange on his white horse. There were several bands as well, some with girls. I liked the ones in the red uniforms with gold buttons on the jackets, straight dark skirts and tall white hats.

The village was closed to traffic, no cars allowed, so I was very surprised when suddenly I heard honking from a little lane a few yards down from us.

Then there was another round of honking, longer than before. Then a third. At this stage the crowd got angry and the shout went up, 'Go back! Go away!'

'Oh dear,' said Dad.

Then I saw. It was our pantechnicon.

Dad rushed over and told the driver of the lorry to stop peeping his horn and then apologised to the crowd. The driver then reversed the lorry back the way he had come, and in so doing he knocked a fence down. The garden on the far side of the fence was filled with pigs and chickens and geese and dogs. The animals scrambled through the hole in the fence, ran up the lane and got mixed up in the parade. Some of the crowd tried to catch the birds and the animals, and before very long bandsmen and onlookers and animals were all colliding with one another. The parade had to be stopped for ten minutes while all the animals were rounded up.

After the parade was finally finished, a man dressed in a uniform came up behind Dad and said, 'What were you doing, trying to sabotage our parade?'

I didn't recognise him at first because he was in his uniform but then I realised who it was from the black eyes; it was Len, the man we'd met on the boat, the man who gave me crisps and a Club biscuit.

I thought Len was angry, but he must have seen my face falling, for then he quickly smiled and said, 'Only joking.'

We went to a refreshment tent pitched on the front lawn of a house, and Len insisted on buying us all tea and hot scones stuffed with raisins.

When we got back to our house, the pantechnicon was parked in the front drive and my younger brother Fred, I noticed, was sitting astride the metal fence near the front door. He had a folded blanket (which must have come from the removal van) for a saddle, and he was firing his cap gun into the air.

I knew I was going to be asked to help, while Fred could do what he wanted; this was unfair, and it made me feel grumpy. I slipped round the side of the house, peered into the conservatory at our piano waiting to be moved inside, and then went through to the back garden without letting Mum see me. There was a rubber tyre attached by a rope to the branch of the big tree. I got on and began to swing, backwards and forwards. As I hung in the air, head back, and looked up at the clouds and the blue sky, and heard the rooks cawing in the trees, I began to feel less grumpy, and less and less grumpy.

'Phoebe, come and help!' Mum shouted from the back door. I could tell she was cross because I wasn't doing anything, but I didn't mind helping now. So I ran in to the kitchen. Mum gave me a tray with mugs of tea and biscuits for the removal men.

'Have you seen Fred?' she asked.

'I saw him on the fence.'

'When?'

'Not long ago.'

'How long?'

'When I got back with Dad from Crookedstone. Before I was on the swing.'

'That was ages ago. Was he annoying the removal men?'

At that moment, two of them were grunting at the

door. 'Nah!' they both called. 'He was playing cow-boys.' They pushed the piano up a ramp and into the kitchen.

'Phoebe, ask Fred to come in and have a biscuit and a drink.'

'I want a biscuit,' said Tom. He was sitting in the corner gazing at the big photographs on the sports pages of Dad's *Guardian*.

'Is that all you can think about?' I said. 'Why don't you help for once? Find Fred! And that's yesterday's paper, duh!'

'Phoebe, that was quite uncalled for,' said Mum. 'You must stop this immediate knee-jerk sarcasm directed against your brothers!'

I went out to the front with the tray and put it in the back of the removal van. The driver went off to round up the other men.

I looked around. There was no sign of Fred, just the blanket draped over the fence and his hat on the ground and his precious gun beside it. How long was it since I'd seen him? Well, I'd probably hung about the con-servatory for a few minutes, and I was on the swing for a long time – half an hour or maybe more. Then I'd gone into the kitchen and talked to Mum and got the tray and carried it out here. So it was near enough fifty minutes since I'd last seen Fred, which was almost an hour, and that was an incredibly long time for a little four year old to be out of our sight.

I picked up his hat and his gun. A big, blue tongue of used caps hung down from the gun. I broke the gun and opened it.

Inside the gun I found a half roll of blue paper with brown blobs like freckles spaced along it. It was half a roll of unused, fresh caps. Now this was very strange. When Fred got a roll of caps, he always did the same thing; he always loaded them in his gun and kept firing until they were all gone. The idea of keeping something and enjoying it several different times, rather than using it all up in one go, was completely unknown to Fred. He was exactly the same with treats. When he got sweets or a bar of chocolate, he couldn't just have a couple of sweets or a couple of squares and then keep the rest for later. Oh no, Fred was the sort of boy who had to eat everything at a sitting.

So if Fred was the sort to fire all his caps off at one go, how come he hadn't this time? As soon as I asked myself this question, my stomach began to tremble. The answer was that something awful had happened. But I didn't want to imagine what exactly this awful thing was. I wanted to keep the idea out of my mind. So as I usually do in these circumstances, I glanced around for something to distract me, or that I could use to keep the thought away.

That was when I saw there was a tractor coming up

our lane. It was old and grey, exactly the same grey as an *Airfix* model. The awful thought was still pressing. In order to keep it out of my mind, I began to do star jumps on the spot. When the tractor got closer, I saw that the driver wore a blue overall and a woollen hat. Then, when the tractor got closer still, I saw that Fred was standing between the driver's knees. He was holding on to the steering wheel. I felt relieved.

Then I looked at my brother's face. I saw that Fred was frightened and happy at the same time. Now it was safe to let the awful thought come into my mind. Because he was alive and kicking I could let it come. What I had feared before was that he had been kid-napped, or worse, hurt, or worse again, killed.

The tractor driver pointed at something and Fred pushed and a horn peeped, very loudly, three times.

Fred laughed and the tractor driver smiled.

Mum came out the front door and Dad stuck his head out of an upstairs window.

'Fred,' Mum shouted, all sort of normal, and then she shouted his name again – 'Fred,' although this time there was something anxious in her voice.

She ran over to the side of the tractor. I ran over and stood behind. I wanted to find out what had happened.

'He's a bit young to be leaving home, so I thought I'd bring him back,' said the driver.

37

He was a man of about forty-five or so, with glasses which he now pushed up his nose.

'What do you mean?'

'I found him on the road, walking along.' Then he rubbed Fred's nose and said, 'Didn't I, son?'

Fred looked down at the ground like he does when he's shy or nervous.

'You were on the main road?' said Mum.

'He'd got quite some way towards town,' said the driver amiably. 'He must have been a mile from here.'

Suddenly, Fred put up his arms and literally flung himself off the tractor and into Mum's arms and began to cry.

'He's got a fright,' said the driver. 'And I don't doubt you must have got one, too.'

He pointed at me. 'You and your dad were round our farm, weren't you?'

I looked at him.

'Last night. The dog was barking and the mother chased you off.'

'Oh yes.'

'I was out at my driving job and the wife and son were away and I'm sorry our Patch wasn't very welcoming and nor was the old mother.'

'It didn't matter,' I said.

'They're neither of them used to strangers but they're good enough underneath.'

He turned the tractor in a circle and crossed the bridge with a wave. There was blue diesel smoke pouring out of a pipe sticking up at the side of the engine.

'Well,' said Mum, holding Fred tightly and rubbing her cheek against his, as we stood there watching the tractor disappearing down our lane. 'There you have a classic example of life in the country. As you will discover, Phoebe, you won't be able to sneeze here but everyone in the neighbourhood will know about it within a few hours.'

'What was all that about?' Dad called from the window.

'Fred decided to leave home, but he changed his mind and now he's back.'

Then she looked at Fred and she whispered, 'You do want to stay with us, Fred, don't you?'

'Yes.'

'You're not going to go wandering off along the main road, are you?'

I heard a muffled, 'No,' and she disappeared with him through the front door, with me following.

It was funny seeing our furniture in the new house. I found it sort of comforting.

Only one thing was lacking, my glass animals – but I didn't have to wait long.

Two days later the postman brought a large brown paper

parcel. As soon as I took it from him, I felt a fizzy feeling underneath my ribs.

I went straight to the kitchen and tore off the paper and opened the box inside. It was filled with wood shavings and sawdust. I plunged my hand in and felt around until I found something hard and shiny. I pulled it up – it was my dolphin. The body is all clear glass with a blue streak down his middle. His back is arched like he's swimming through the sea.

Then I felt this stab. It was a sharp pain and it hurt. It was in me, right in my middle, where the fizzing had been. Then I got this raw feeling at the back of my throat. I wasn't going to be able to stop myself so I just let go. I started to cry. But I went on pulling out all my other glass animals at the same time. Where the tears plopped on the table, the wood changed colour from light to dark.

I heard the door opening and next I heard Mum saying, 'What's the matter? What is it, Phoebe?'

I ran over to her and threw my arms around her and put my face on her stomach.

I cried for a long time. She told me not to be sad. Then she said, 'Would you like to come swimming? That would be a nice thing to do, wouldn't it? Get us out of here.'

'Yes,' I said.

5 I meet Emma

I whooshed down the slide and landed in the water. No big deal. The slide wasn't very high and the water wasn't very deep. I got out and queued up and went down again. It was actually quite a tame slide. I thought about swimming over to Mum to tell her that I thought even Fred would be able to do it. But instead I decided to have a third go because three is my lucky number, and then I would go over.

At the back of the slide I found myself behind a very fat boy. He was cold and as he shivered his skin sort of bounced. When his turn came he climbed up the ladder, sat at the top of the slide and froze.

'What's up, Clive?' asked a woman in a plastic bathing hat.

She was fat too. I guessed she was his mother.

'Umh.' Clive opened and closed his mouth. I wanted to say, get off or get on with it.

His mother said, 'Hold my hand and I'll slide you down, all right?'

This was taking ages and I was about to give up when suddenly Clive pushed himself forward. Half a second later he shot off the end of the slide and sank like a stone. Then he stood up and punched the air like a footballer who has just scored. It was nauseating. I hurried up the steps and sat down at the top of the slide. Next thing, I was shooting off the end of the slide. I still had my eyes on Clive and I realised that something was wrong. My body was sort of twisted. I had to straighten up. So I jerked my neck. My head came forward. I lost control. My mouth hit my knee and I felt something splinter. Then I was in the water. I looked up. Everything was fuzzy. There was a terrible pain in my gum. I found the floor with my foot and stood and let out a cry. There was blood streaming from my mouth. It tasted of metal. The life guard had jumped in to the water. I saw him lurch towards me. I put my palm over my mouth and felt something fall. I opened my hand and looked down. I saw a small, jagged, white triangle. It was a piece of my front tooth.

Half an hour later we were all in the dentist's waiting room, Mum, the two boys and me.

A woman came in with a girl and they sat down opposite us. They were mother and daughter, all right. They had the same heart-shaped faces, the same bright blue eyes.

Mum smiled and the woman said, 'Hello,' and Mum said, 'Hello,' back, and the woman said, 'What brought you here?' because Mum's accent wasn't local, and within seconds the two of them were rabbiting on. The woman was called Linda, her daughter was called Emma, and Mum had soon gathered that this Emma was at the very school that I was going to start in September.

'How old are you, Emma?' she asked.

'Eleven.'

'You'll be in the same class.' Mum said this excitedly. Then she added, 'Phoebe's going to be eleven any minute now. September 3rd.'

'Oh no, that's after term starts,' said Emma. She looked at me in a caring, concerned, interested way.

'Is it?' I said.

'Not that it matters,' she said quickly. 'You can have your party any time you want, and you are having a party, aren't you?'

I ran my tongue over the broken tooth edge as I considered the question and enjoyed the attention.

'Phoebe!' Mum nudged me.

'Oh, sorry. Yes, I suppose we will, won't we, Mum?' I said.

'Oh yes, we'll do something. You can't miss out on the big one,' said Mum firmly. Then Mum said, 'I think the 3rd is a Thursday this year, and school starts on the Tuesday before, doesn't it?' Linda said she thought this was right, and then the two grown-ups started talking about something else. I looked across at Emma and she looked back at me. She had freckles on her nose and a pointed chin. Somehow or other, our mums got on to smoking and the difficulties of giving up. As they vied to cap each other's stories, their talk grew wilder and wilder. At some point Emma rolled her eyes at their excited chatter and that was when it happened.

It felt like gears clicking together and a machine coming to life inside me. Here was the friend I needed, and she was sitting on the other side of a dentist's waiting room, underneath a poster of a talking toothbrush called Sammy the Plaque Buster.

I also realised something else at this moment.

The friend Mum needed was on the other side of the waiting room as well. This meeting was the best thing to have happened since we came to Crookedstone, and if I hadn't broken my tooth it might never have happened.

Then a nurse in a white gown put her head round the door and said, 'Phoebe Rodgers, come through,' in a bossy voice.

I was injected and drilled. The dentist put a tiny bar in the front tooth and used that to hold the broken corner in place. When he finished he said dentistry was the eighth wonder of the world. I couldn't speak. So I just nodded.

I came out. Mum and Linda were still chatting away. It sounded as if they'd known each other all their lives, and I had to remind myself it was more like forty minutes.

'My turn for the torture chamber,' said Emma, standing.

She lifted her arms and began to stagger woodenly, like Frankenstein. I laughed, which was difficult, as half my face was frozen by the anaesthetic.

'You know that your house is very close to where we live,' said Linda.

'I think they're cooking something up,' muttered Emma in Frankenstein's voice. 'They think it's a good idea to be friends.'

She fiddled with the bolt at the side of her throat and rolled her eyes. I forgot my frozen face and laughed again.

'Why don't you both come to tea after this?' said Mum. 'I've some toffee apples at home and I'm sure the girls would love to watch us eat them.'

Linda clapped her hands. 'At last, someone with my sense of humour,' she called, and Emma staggered in to the surgery.

Later, Mum said, 'Why don't you take Emma upstairs and show her your room?'

We were in the kitchen, and we'd just had five

minutes of Mum and Linda going 'ooh and ah' over the Sheila Maid, the old Aga, the pine cupboards, the quarry tiles, the Belfast sink, the dado rail. They were getting on well, so well in fact, I reckoned the cogs in Mum had meshed with Linda, exactly as mine had with Emma.

But then, she and Linda had a lot in common. Like a sense of humour. And a love of Habitat catalogues. And they both wanted to go back to smoking but couldn't because their children wouldn't let them.

'Don't just sit there like a lazy lump,' Linda chided her daughter. 'Make a bit of an effort.'

Emma had her back to her mother, her face to me, and as Linda spoke she mouthed the words, *Don't sit there like a lazy lump! Make a bit of an effort!* I thought it was really funny the way she could take her mother off. Really funny.

'Tell you what,' she said, looking right at me, 'let's go out and we'll take, umh . . .'

She was trying to remember the boy's names.

'Fred and Tom.'

'We'll take Fred and Tom,' she continued.

The boys, who were hovering nearby, cried, 'Yes.'

'I'll take you all to see the donkey and maybe we might have a look at a place to build a base,' continued Emma.

'Oh wow! A base,' the boys shouted. This was going

to earn me so many Brownie points from Mum.

Emma took us up the track at the back of our house, over the hill and down into the valley behind. We stopped at the fence of a large green field. On the far side there were cows grazing beside a hawthorn hedge. And a few yards away there was a donkey chewing the grass.

'Come on, Socks!' she called over to him.

He was the colour of coal, with little white feet and pointed grey ears.

'Socks!' she called again. The donkey looked up and slowly started to amble towards us.

'Tear up some grass,' ordered Emma, and the boys pulled a handful each and reached over the fence in Socks' direction. The donkey saw but he didn't change his pace. He just ambled on, exactly as before and finally he came to a halt a few feet back from the fence.

'He's a very stupid donkey. Throw the grass over,' Emma ordered.

'Won't he eat it from my hand?' wailed a disappointed Fred.

'I've been coming for years to see him and this is the only way he'll eat anything.'

The boys threw their clumps of grass and dandelions into the field, where they formed a little pile. Socks bent down and snorted, his nose opening and closing, and then he took a small, shy mouthful.

'Let's have a ride,' said Emma. 'He's perfectly safe. I've been up on him a thousand times at least.'

We climbed over the gate and walked up to Socks. He did not look up at us but stared down at the ground while slowly chewing.

'Upsy-daisy.'

Emma lifted first Tom and then Fred on to Socks' furry back. Still the donkey did not move but just stayed as he was, frozen, except for his grinding jaw.

'And that's the height of it,' explained Emma. 'You can sit on him all day, but Socks does not and will not budge. Not an inch.'

Suddenly, without warning, Socks stretched his neck forward, bared his teeth and brayed. I jumped out of my skin and my brothers leapt off the donkey and ran back to us with pale faces. I was about to call out, 'Scaredy cats, scaredy cats,' but before I could get the words out, Emma had an arm over each shoulder.

'His bray is worse than his bite,' she joked.

The boys said nothing, just stood there and stared at Socks' open mouth, the yellow teeth sticking out of his purple gums, the tendons in his neck standing up under his skin like lengths of rope.

Eventually he stopped braying and went back to chewing slowly. Emma nodded towards the grey slate roof of a house peeping out from some trees in the distance.

'That's where we live,' she said. The lane that we had come up was a quick way between our two houses, and one that avoided the main roads.

'So,' continued Emma, 'with us living so close, we'll just have to go with the flow and be friends as our mothers want.'

She was funny, and because of the way she had put her arms around my brothers, I knew that she was kind, as well.

'All right,' I said. It sounded like a great idea to me.

We sealed our friendship, Emma and I, by building a base for the boys inside the rhododendron bush that grows on the far side of the house; corrugated iron for the roof; a pallet covered with a square of lino for the floor; planks for walls and bald tyres for seats inside.

As a final touch, we found some old whiskey bottles in an outhouse and tied them by string to the branches. When the breeze blew, they clinked against one another.

That was my idea, my only contribution, in fact. It was Emma who did the designing, while I did the donkey work. But I didn't mind. Emma had a way of telling me what to do that didn't get my back up. She was polite but, more importantly, she let me know it was just for now that I was doing this for her, and next time, she was the one who would run backwards and forwards while I told her what to do. That's what it seemed like, anyway, at the time.

We finished and sat on the rhododendron branches, listening to the clinking bottles, while the boys hooted and hollered inside the base, and then Mum and Linda came out to see how we'd done.

'Wonderful,' said Mum.

'It's amazing what children can improvise,' said Linda. They'd already had a couple of glasses of wine. I could see Mum was delighted and a little excited. I had a friend. She had a friend. 'Linda's staying the night and Emma can stay in your room,' she announced.

There were wonderful clouds that evening. They were like great big pillows in the sky. As the sun sank they went purple, and the edges went gold. I took Emma up to my room.

'Bare walls, very sad,' said Emma.

I hadn't got my posters up yet. So I took them out of their cardboard tube and spread them on the bed; I had one of Kermit the frog, one for the book *Going Solo* with a picture of Roald Dahl in the corner, one showing a puppy in the middle of a load of pink Andrex toilet tissue, one of the groovy five, Take That, and a wanted poster for Dad offering a $5000 reward. We began to stick them up with Plastitack trying them on this wall, trying them on that wall (it's always very hard to get posters in the right place) and as we worked away, I heard myself saying, 'Tell me the story of your life,' and Emma said, 'All right.'

'Linda was a hippie,' she began. 'You know, she wore long skirts and went around in bare feet. That's if it wasn't raining, of course. Anyway, she decided she was going to India. So she got on the ferry at Larne to go across to Scotland – she had to go to London, you see, to catch this bus that was going to take her to India – and on the ferry she met Dermot – he worked on the boat as a deck hand – and Linda and Dermot got talking. When they got to Stranraer, they walked off the boat, still talking, and went on to India together on this bus. It was 'The Purple Bus' and it was purple on the inside as well. Then they came back to Belfast and I was born.'

'And where's Dermot now?' I wondered.

'Well, after I was born,' continued Emma, 'Dermot went back to India. Then he came back. But not to Ireland, to Scotland. And that's where he lives now. He's working as a guard on the railways at the moment, and he's saving up to go travelling again.'

'Do you ever see him?'

'Oh yes. I've been over to see him in Scotland, twice. He's very nice. He treats me well. One night he took me to Sauchiehall Street. Do you know what that is?'

'No.'

'It's the main street in Glasgow.'

'Like Oxford Street in London?' I said

'Well, I suppose, I don't know. But the point is, when we were in Sauchiehall Street, he took me into four different places and I had four different ice-creams in one evening.'

Then she stopped and gazed at the poster she was putting up. It was the one of Dad in a cowboy hat that looked like a poster in a cowboy film and said *Wanted – Dangerous Dave Rodgers – Reward $5000.00.*

'Of course, he's never going to marry Linda,' she said.

I loved the story, it was incredibly exciting, all except the end, of course. Dermot should have stayed, because in a good story that's what would have happened. Also, it was much better having a father than not. Whenever Mum was cross with me, my dad always bought me chocolate or something, and when he was cross, she did the same. That was the point of two parents. One was nice when the other was horrible. However, I decided not to share these thoughts at that moment.

Instead I said, 'Don't you miss him?'

'Not a bit.'

'Why?'

'Oh, if he lived with us, he'd hog the TV and he'd

leave his socks lying all round the house.'

I didn't believe she actually meant this.

'That can't be right,' I said.

I just thought she was trying to impress me. She was just repeating what she'd heard Linda say, I guessed.

'What about treats and trips and things?' I said. 'For them, at least, wouldn't you like your dad around?'

There was a very long pause. I knew this meant she would tell the truth now.

Finally she spoke: 'What you want and what you have are two quite separate things,' said Emma, smoothing a crease on Kermit's nose. 'Dermot doesn't believe in commitment, you see, and he loves to travel, and we don't fit in with his plans.'

I didn't know what to reply and luckily, that was the moment when Mum called up, 'Supper!'

When we got down we found candles burning on the table – 'They're in honour of our guests,' said Mum – and a vast bowl filled with *salade Niçoise*.

'And it's got real, fresh parsley from the garden,' said Mum excitedly. 'Linda spotted some. It was growing in a bed at the back.'

'Well spotted, eagle eyes,' said Dad, pulling up a chair.

The grown-ups seemed in very good humour as we

sat down, and Emma whispered in my ear, 'They've been drinking.'

'Whispering's rude! Don't whisper!' shouted Linda. 'What did you say?'

'Nothing,' said Emma.

'No, I want to know what you said.'

'Nothing. I didn't say anything about you. And don't be so nosy.'

'Oh come on. No one around this table believes that.' Then Linda looked straight at my dad and said, 'Do you believe my darling daughter?'

I had a funny feeling about Linda's questions. I didn't like the way she'd gone on and on. But when she said, 'darling daughter,' that made my dad laugh, and then everyone laughed.

'No, your darling daughter wasn't saying nothing,' my dad replied.

'So,' said Linda. 'What were you saying?' She made her question sound jokey but this wasn't a joke.

'You've been drinking,' said Emma. 'That's what I said.'

The adults laughed again.

'From now on I want to hear everything you say,' said Linda. 'I like to know exactly what's going on in the heads of you cunning children. No plots or schemes or gossiping behind my back. I want to know everything. Understood?'

'See what I mean,' said Emma. 'She's mad.'

More laughter, and I joined in this time. Yet something wasn't right about what Linda had just said, although I couldn't put my finger on it and say exactly what it was.

I began to eat. There were anchovies in the salad and I don't like anchovies. I picked them out and pushed them to the side of my plate.

'Oh, I'll have them,' said Emma. 'I love anchovies and olives, anything salty.'

'It's all down to the pregnancy,' said Linda, 'at least that's what I believe. I was on a boat at the time I was pregnant with her, going down the coast of India. I had salt and spray and sea all around me for three months, and that gave her that love of salty things. I'm sure of it.'

'Was that with Dermot?' I asked Emma quietly.

'My goodness! You haven't wasted any time,' said Linda smiling. 'So you've told your new friend all about Dermot and everything?'

'Not everything,' said Emma.

I was blushing a bit, and from the way she wriggled on her seat beside me, so was Emma.

'She's so sweet,' continued Linda, and pointed to Emma. 'At school they were doing a project on the family and everyone had a sheet and they had to write down their family details and she wrote under

"Type" – "Single parent family and proud of it." '

'Linda,' said Emma, 'please.'

'A bit of praise never did a child any harm,' said Linda. She turned to Mum and Dad. 'Wouldn't you agree?'

The grown-ups began to talk amongst themselves, and a few minutes later, when we'd finished eating, we left the table.

I woke the next morning. A band of bright sunlight lay across the ceiling above. Emma was in the other bed and I heard the regular in and out of her breathing.

I took my diary out of the drawer of the bedside locker and wrote down under the day before's date: *Made my first Northern Ireland friend, Emma Turtle. She's not like Sylvia. When S and I are with one another, we dream together. With Emma I don't dream. I talk. I laugh. My horrible brothers love Emma. They become quite well-behaved when they are near her. It's amazing. Emma's mother is called Linda and she is nice too, but also a bit weird (I think). It's as if the person underneath her words is hard and a bit frightening.* I wrote all this quickly, without thinking. I didn't want Emma to wake up and see me writing.

I hid the diary under my pillow and snuggled back down under the duvet. It was warm and I felt drowsy and happy. I looked down at Emma's face. It was very wide at the top, tapering to a chin with a dimple in the middle. That chin was the first thing I had noticed about her, that and the freckles on her nose. As I looked at her now, I saw that she also had a few freckles on each cheek, and on the forehead which I could see under her fringe, and even on her eyelids. Her black hair lay spread out on the pillow underneath her head.

She looked a bit like the dormouse in *Alice in Wonderland*, I thought, when she was asleep. But awake, she was like a cat, very watchful.

'What are you looking at?' she said, suddenly opening her eyes.

'Nothing in particular,' I said, which was the truth.

She didn't go from sleeping to waking, slowly. Not like me.

'Do you want to see something?'

'What?'

'My special skill?'

'What?'

'I can't tell you,' she said. 'I can only show you.'

'All right.'

'Get me a pencil and paper.'

'Why?'

'Just get a pencil and paper.'

I got a big pad of A4 paper and a pencil from the locker beside my bed.

'Now write something,' she said.

'What?'

'Anything.'

'Why?'

'Just write.'

'Anything?'

'Yeah.'

Dad practices his typing by writing *The quick brown fox jumps over the lazy dog.* It uses all the letters of the alphabet. So I wrote it out in joined-up writing.

'Now write that again,' said Emma, when I'd finished.

She made me do it twice more and then she got me to sign my name a few times.

'Okey-dokey,' she said, took the pad and the pencil from me, and studied the page intently. Finally, she put the pencil on the paper and slowly began to copy *The quick brown fox jumps over the lazy dog. Phoebe Rodgers* in my writing.

'What do you think?' she said when she finished, and handed me the pad.

It was amazing. She had copied my handwriting exactly, every loop and curl and squiggle of it.

'Mum broke her wrist last year. It was in plaster for a month. It was her right wrist and she's right-handed. So I learnt how to do her signature and sign her cheques and that. Pretty impressive, isn't it?'

I nodded. It really was.

'I've toyed with the idea of becoming a master forger,' she said, 'but in the end, I decided crime doesn't pay.'

'Have you got any friends?' I asked.

'Well of course I have.'

'What are their names?'

'Belladonna and Smellychump.'

'What?'

'Only joking. Nicola and Sarah. You'll meet 'em. They're nice.' She yawned and stretched. 'I'm nicer, though.'

There was silence. Just bird song outside and a cow in the distance, and the television downstairs. The boys were watching it.

'I can do Mr Dong, the headmaster's signature,' said Emma. 'Whenever a notice goes up round the school I always make a point of signing it *Ding Dong, your headmaster*. That's if no teachers are looking.'

I laughed. Then I noticed she was staring over at me without smiling. 'Terribly childish but it keeps the younger ones amused,' she drawled like an actress.

'You mean Nicola and Sarah?'

'Oh no, they're my age,' (which I realised, of course, as soon as my stupid question was out). 'I'm talking about the twits at the bottom of the school. The six-year-olds, the ones who roar with laughter even when you just say, "Ding Dong".'

'They're your friends, Nicola and Sarah?'

'That's right.'

What were they like? I wanted to know everything. And would they be my friends? Would they like me? Or would I spend the rest of the holidays making friends with Emma, only to find when I got to school in September and she had Nicola and Sarah again, that she didn't want to know me any more?

'I'll meet them then,' I said, trying to sound interested but not eager.

'Oh yeah. Don't worry.' She said this in her actress voice again. 'I could murder a slice of bacon, you know.'

Downstairs, Linda was sitting at the table in the kitchen. She was wearing a pair of dark glasses. Mum was by the stove laying strips of bacon on the grill.

'Morning, girls, how about some bacon?' said Mum.

'You know, you read my mind. I just said to Phoebe upstairs, I'd love a slice of bacon.'

'It's the best cure for too much whiskey,' said Mum.

She was happy. She was very, very happy indeed. I could tell.

Everything was going to be all right.

6 School

Later that morning, Linda and Emma went off home, and Mum took me into town and we got my school uniform; a blue smock with a green sash which tied around the middle, grey shirt, black and green tie, grey socks, dark shoes.

When I got home I went up to my bedroom and put the uniform on straight away. This was my first ever school uniform and I was excited.

I went downstairs to the kitchen.

'Oh, you look lovely,' said Mum.

Even the baby Fred said, 'Nice uniform.'

'Let's take a picture,' said Mum. 'Come on.'

Outside the sun was shining. She put me standing on the wall and put herself on the ground immediately underneath me.

'Look down at the camera,' she said.

Next evening she stuck several photographs of me in the new uniform into the scrap album she'd started called *Coming to Fermanagh*. Underneath the pictures of me she wrote a few words in blue ink, as she always did in her albums:

Wednesday 26th August, 1992. Phoebe – looking rather fetching I think – in her new school uniform; she is standing outside our house on a blazing late August day. Next week she starts her new primary school and another part of our new life in Ireland will be underway.

*

The first day of term was a Tuesday. We all got in the car, myself and the boys, and Mum.

'It's your big day, here at last,' said Mum, as we drove down our lane.

The boys were happy. Fred would start at the school in a year's time, lucky beggar, while Tom, who was seven, would start the next day, when he would join the P3 class.

We drove along the road. The boys talked, Mum talked. I heard nothing, saw nothing. My stomach was all knots. Who would talk to me? I'd seen Emma, of course, a few times since the first night she came to stay. And on the Sunday, the one just gone, Dad had taken the two of us to the skating rink at Dundonald, and afterwards we had gone for pizzas in Belfast, and after that he'd taken us to Maud's for ice-cream. This was my birthday treat. I always got on with Emma. She was my friend. But at school she'd be with Nicola and Sarah. They were her old friends. She might be different when they were around. She might be cool with me. She might forget she'd shared my birthday treat. She might ignore me, for goodness sake. She might want nothing to do with me.

Then the pictures started in my head and I couldn't stop them.

I imagined myself sitting in the class, the only child with no one at the desk beside them. Next, I imagined myself eating school dinner, alone again. And finally, I imagined myself in the playground, squeezed against the wall, while children shouted and chased all around me.

We arrived, finally, at the Farmer's Memorial school, and stopped in the car park outside the gates. I had an impression of cars, grown-ups bustling, children scampering, everyone shouting.

'Right,' said Mum. She released her safety belt and jumped out. My brothers followed her. Here was 'New Girl's Dilemma, number 101'. What was worse – that I walked through the gates by myself, or that I went in with my family? Well, I decided, at least I could pretend to talk to them.

I got out and we all began to walk forward in a line. I had taken Fred and Tom's hands without realising what I was doing. The embarrassment. I must disentangle myself, I thought, but before I was able to, I heard, 'Hello, Phoebe.'

It was not a voice I recognised. I looked up and saw a girl with dark curly hair, an even face, and three large interesting looking moles on her left cheek. Nicola, I thought. She had moles. Moley, she was sometimes called. Emma had told me this.

'I'm Nicola,' she said.

At that point my mind went absolutely blank and my throat stopped working.

'And this is our sister, Phoebe,' shouted Tom and Fred in their little boy voices.

I saw children and parents turning round. I could have died.

'I know. I guessed who it was,' said Nicola. 'There's only one new girl in our class this year, and you're the only new face here, so I knew it had to be you. I'm a friend of Emma's, you know.'

'Oh.'

Nicola began to move along the path. There were two buildings ahead. I could see the playground between the buildings and children flashing across the space.

I let go of Tom and Fred's hands and made a flapping movement with my own hands.

'We'll go. See you tonight,' said Mum, ever tactful.

The family vanished and it was just Nicola and myself.

'This is school,' she said. 'It's OK.' She paused. 'If you like school.'

I laughed.

'Do you like school?' she asked.

I tried to think of something clever to say but in the end all I managed was, 'I don't know.'

'Oh, I think it's OK,' she said. 'Tough year, though.'

'Yeah!' Obviously she was talking about the exam, the Eleven Plus. This decided whether you went on to grammar school, or secondary school. Dad had had several long conversations with me about it, none of which I had really taken in. I do know he wanted me to pass. I was clear about that. He wanted me to go to grammar school.

'Yeah,' Nicola said, which agreed with my yeah.

Perhaps she meant the school itself, the pupils, the teachers were tough?

'Yeah,' I said again. Now I was agreeing with her yeah. If we went on like this, our conversation would soon grind to a halt.

Thank goodness, at that moment, another girl came up, small build, chestnut-coloured hair and lovely chestnut-coloured eyes.

'This is Sarah,' said Nicola.

'Hello, Phoebe,' said Sarah.

I nodded at Sarah and said hello back. Non-chalantly, though. Inside I was dead pleased; here were Emma's best friends and they were talking to me.

'You know Emma?' I said.

'Yeah,' she said.

Oh great. Back to the yeahs again.

'If we want to sit together, we'd better bag our desk,' said Nicola.

Was this addressed to Sarah, or was I included? I didn't want to seem eager, but I didn't want them to ignore me either, so I just said, 'Where's our classroom?'

'Come on, we'll show you. You can help.'

They began to hurry across the asphalt, through the screeching children, and I followed.

'Oh goodness,' shouted Sarah. 'Alert! Alert! Caretaker.'

I saw a big man lolloping towards us, a ball under his arm. He was followed by a small crowd of tiny boys and he was shouting, 'Come on, follow Mr Finch, and he'll give you goals, boys.'

'Good morning, girls,' the caretaker called over to us. Sarah smiled at the caretaker. We formed a pretend huddle. Mr Finch swept on.

'Right, he's gone.'

We bolted through swing doors. Inside I found myself in a corridor which smelt of wax, Plasticine, and dimly of disinfectant.

'On the right,' shouted Nicola.

We darted through a door with Miss Ferguson written on it, and I found myself in a big room crowded with desks.

'Right,' said Nicola. 'I think here will do nicely.'

She moved four desks and joined them together. Her chosen spot was a good distance from the front but not so far back as to attract Miss Ferguson's attention or annoy her.

'Come on. Get your bags unpacked, you two. We've got to make these ours.'

'I haven't got anything,' I said.

'Just put your bag on the desk you want.' This was Sarah.

So I was in.

At that moment, someone rapped on the window and shouted, 'What are you doing in there? You know you're not allowed in the classrooms before first bell.'

I was sure I was in trouble, only it turned out it was Emma, and she had a big grin on her face.

'What time do you call this?' Sarah pointed at her wrist.

'Yeah, what time do you call this?' repeated Nicola.

A horrible smile, simpering and sickly, suddenly appeared on Emma's face. It didn't suit her.

'Yeah, what time do you call this?' I chorused, pointing at my Mickey Mouse watch.

Emma shook her head, and just as I realised she was warning us, a voice behind said, 'I call it five to nine and as you know perfectly well, Nicola and Emma, you are not allowed in until first bell.'

I turned. There was Miss Ferguson. Blonde hair, nice face, fawn-coloured jacket and skirt, a white blouse underneath, crisp and starched.

'I see you don't waste any time before corrupting the innocent,' she said. 'Please take Phoebe Rodgers outside and stay outside until first bell.'

Then she looked at me.

'It would be far better, Phoebe, if you didn't associate with these reprobates, but as I know they're a great deal of fun, I can't imagine you'll listen to me.'

We ran through the door, along the corridor and out into the playground, and there, with a great sense of release, we all roared with laughter.

The bell went. Emma and the other two showed me the drill. Everyone lined up in the playground. We trooped inside. As soon as I came into the classroom I could feel everyone looking at me. My face went bright red, my ears as well, and I tried to pay no attention. But it was pretty painless really, as were the other first-day-at-school ordeals. I just followed Emma, Nicola and Sarah around. I didn't try to talk to them much, I didn't try to make out I was funny. I just listened to them talking.

Miss Ferguson gave us a big lecture. In two months time, she said, we would sit the Transfer Test, as the Eleven Plus was called; two papers, one hour each, seventy-five questions on each paper. Twenty-five per cent of those who sat the exam would get an A; they would go on to grammar school. The rest didn't. It was as simple as that. That was Miss Ferguson's favourite phrase. 'It's as simple as that, girls and boys, it's as simple as that.'

At the end of the day, Miss Ferguson asked me to stay behind. She came and sat at the desk beside me. She wore nice perfume and her hair was clean. She ran through a test paper with me, showed me the different types of questions, and then set me a couple of pages of questions to do myself, there and then.

It didn't take me long to finish the pages, and I handed the paper back to her. I mostly got the questions right, and Miss Ferguson put big ticks in pencil in the margin.

'There won't be any trick questions, Phoebe,' she said. 'The transfer test isn't that kind of an exam. With the transfer test, you either know the answers because you've done the work, or you don't know the answers because you haven't done the work. You're a bright girl, but you'll have to work if you're going to catch up with the rest of us, but I think you'll manage easily. I'm going to give you a book of test papers to take home. The answers are in the back. I want you to do two one hour papers a week. Do you think you can do that?'

'Yes,' I said.

'Here it is, then. When you do a paper, do it as if it

were for real. Have your mum or dad time you, get them to mark the questions. I've written a note for them which is inside the book explaining everything. Will you give it to them?'

I said, 'Yes.'

'All right, Phoebe, you'd better go. I've kept you back long enough.'

She gave me a lovely smile. I ran out. I found Mum in the car park, chatting away to Linda and Emma.

'I gotta do a whole load of Transfer Test papers,' I groaned.

'Quite right,' said Linda. 'You want to go to grammar school, you have to do the work.'

The next day Mum brought myself and Tom to school. He was a bit anxious; he wanted Mum to stay with him in the playground. But I didn't want to hang around, so I found Emma.

That night, Tom wet his bed. He didn't want Mum to know about it, so he came and woke me up. I had to change him, and his bed, and then he got in to my bed anyway. Lovely. He made me promise that when we started going to school on the bus, instead of with Mum, I'd stay with him in the playground. To my complete amazement, I heard myself saying yes.

I loved school, because from the moment I stepped through the gate, I had three good friends. We were inseparable. What was more, the other children liked us, and they envied us at the same time. I was popular. I was happy. And I was really glad we'd left London and come here.

The first weekend I did four test papers, two on Saturday, two on Sunday. By the second day, my scores were edging above seventy percent.

On Monday morning, at breakfast, I said to Mum, 'Didn't I do well?' and she said, 'Indeed you did, darling.' Then she continued, 'Do you want me to bring you in, or do you want to take the school bus?'

Tom looked at me. I looked at Tom and nodded.

'I'll stay with you in the playground, Tom,' I said. 'I promised you I would and I will.'

Of course, the problem wasn't Tom, it was Mum. She wanted to bring us in. I could tell from the way she asked the question.

Nicola was on the same route as we were, and I'd promised Nicola, on Friday, that I'd see her on the bus on Monday. So the last thing I wanted was to break my word, go in by car, and turn up at school with Mum in tow.

But I didn't want to hurt her feelings either.

'You don't really want to bring us in, do you?' I said. 'Do you?'

Half an hour later, I walked down the lane with Tom at my side. We stopped at the end of the lane and I looked along the main road. A couple of cars zipped past and then I saw the big, yellow school bus hurtling towards us. The driver stopped with a squeal of brakes and the door at the side of the bus opened with a hiss.

'Hello,' said the driver. He was resting his chest on the wheel. 'What's your name?'

'Phoebe Rodgers.'

'And who's that beside you?'

'Tom Rodgers,' said my brother.

'Hop on. I know who you are.'

I turned round without thinking what I was doing, and that was when I saw that Mum had followed us. She was standing on our bridge, looking down our lane at us, Fred beside her. I tapped Tom and he turned and saw. Mum was wearing her red dress and so it was easy to see her in the distance. She gave us a huge wave.

I waved back, Tom waved, we ran up the steps and the doors of the bus hissed shut behind us. And there was Nicola.

'Here, Phoebe,' she shouted, waving me over with a magazine. I ran down the aisle and sat beside her. Tom came up, thought about getting on my lap, and then thought better of it and got into the seat behind us.

'Any news?' said Nicola.

I felt warm inside because Mum had waved to me. This was much better than following me down and hugging me.

'No news,' I said.

We started idly talking about our day, and forty bumpy minutes later we arrived at school. When we got into the playground, we found Emma waiting there. For once, Linda had got Emma in early.

'Hello,' I said.

'Hopscotch?' she said.

We ran over to the grid painted on the asphalt. Tom as well.

'What's he doing?' Emma asked.

I explained.

'OK, Tom,' said Emma, 'your job is to make certain no one steps on the lines. Can you manage that?'

He said yes.

When we got into class, we couldn't stop talking for some reason. Miss Ferguson asked the 'Chattering Four' (as she now referred to us) to stop talking several times. She split us up, made each of us sit at different desks with other children. But we were all so excited, we couldn't stop ourselves. Eventually, Miss Ferguson sent us off to see the headmaster.

'Ding, dong, ding, dong,' Emma chanted, as we walked the corridor towards his office, our shoes squeaking on the linoleum floor. Mr Dong was not amused with our account of our behaviour. He set us all lines. I had to write out two hundred times: *I must not talk to Emma, Sarah and Nicola.*

In the evening, when I showed Mum the lines, she exploded. She said, 'How ridiculous, setting lines!'

'Yeah, well,' said Dad, looking up from the newspaper he was reading in the corner, 'you don't get one thing without the other.'

'What are you talking about?' said Mum.

'This place is stuck in a time warp, circa nineteen fifty. Look, it's like this. We can bring our children to the cinema in town, for instance, and leave them there for the afternoon, and know that nothing will happen to them, can't we? Now we couldn't do that in London, could we? But there's a price to pay. If you want an old-fashioned world where you can leave your children at the cinema, then you have to accept that everything else will be old-fashioned as well. The Transfer Test, which is really the old Eleven Plus, is part of the old-fashioned quality of this place, and giving out lines is another.'

I sat down and began writing. It was incredibly boring. As I wrote, I started thinking about my old school in London, St. Dominic's, and then I was struck by the fact that I hadn't thought about it at all until now. It was as if I'd always lived in Crookedstone and always gone to the Farmer's Memorial.

That, in turn, led me to think about Sylvia. I hadn't thought about her either. I was awful; my best friend and I hadn't thought about her once since I got here. As soon as I finished the lines, I wrote to her.

I felt funny about this letter. The fact was, I was having a brilliant time. I adored Emma, Nicola and Sarah, and I was worried if I said too much about them, she'd be jealous or hurt. So I played things down a bit, but I didn't lie. If I lied, how would I explain to Sylvia if she came out who Emma, Nicola and Sarah were?

I showed Mum the letter. She said it was great. I sent it off. Sylvia sent me back a postcard of a red London bus. She said she missed me, she wanted to see me, that sort of thing. I put it in my drawer, and from time to time I would get it out and re-read it.

7 The test and after

It was a November morning, very cold and very grey. The Farmer's Memorial school was closed to all the children except those in P7 taking the Transfer Test. Mum brought me to school that morning – she wouldn't let me take the bus – and when she pulled up outside the gates, there were only a couple of cars parked up.

I said goodbye and, with my pen and my pencil case and my ruler, I went through to the playground. I found Emma, Nicola and Sarah standing in a corner, sheltering from the wind. I gave each of them a homemade card with *Go for broke and break a leg* scrawled inside. They all got exactly the same message as I knew they would compare cards.

Miss Ferguson rang the bell and we trooped in to our assembly hall-cum-gymnasium. The stack chairs were gone, the piano was in the corner, and on the wooden floor which had a badminton court marked up on it, three lines of desks were laid out.

We each had a number and we had to sit at the desk which corresponded to the number. My place was in the middle row, right at the front. The invigilator handed round the papers. He said a few words then gave the signal to start.

Every time I came to a question I was not able to answer, I moved on rather than wasting time struggling with it. When I came to the end of the paper, I went back to the start and tried to answer all the questions I wasn't able to answer before, like Miss Ferguson had taught us.

After an hour, the invigilator told us to put down our pens.

We went out into the yard where a drizzle fell from a grey sky. We gathered round Miss Ferguson. We showed her the paper. We all decided it was a particularly difficult one; this was apparently a 'good thing' as the harder the paper, the more lenient the marking was likely to be. Maureen Stubbs cried quietly in the corner, certain she had failed.

Two weeks later we did another exam. Then there was nothing else to do but sit back and wait for the results.

In February, the letter came to say I had passed the Transfer Test. I had expected it would be an incredibly impressive letter but it turned out to be a quite ordinary one which simply said I had got an A. I got straight on the phone to Emma. She had passed; so had Nicola and Sarah. We'd all got through.

Now it had to be decided where I was going to go.

Mum and Dad visited the two grammar schools for girls – the controlled school and the maintained school. The controlled school is the Enniskillen Girls Academy, and the maintained school is Our Lady of Fatima. The Academy is a Protestant school, and Our Lady is a Catholic school.

'Why are there two types of school which teach exactly the same things?' I asked Dad on the way back from the open night at Our Lady of Fatima.

'Because of 1690,' he said.

'You're just confusing her,' said Mum, who was sitting beside him in the front of the car. 'That's just a date. It doesn't mean anything to her.'

I knew what the date meant.

'Because of the Battle of the Boyne,' he said.

Which I knew. The mystery was why there was so much anger about it, still, three hundred years later.

'That doesn't mean anything to her either,' said Mum, which were my own thoughts entirely.

'It's because of bitterness,' said Dad bluntly.

'What does an eleven-year-old know about bitterness?' said Mum. 'You know so much about it, why can't you find some way of getting it across to her. Why can't you explain to her what happened?'

'Ye-ah, Dad,' I said.

'I'll give her a reading list,' quipped Dad, 'will that be all right, Madame?'

'I don't know why you can't be more of a teacher,' said Mum, shaking her head.

'Because I'm not a teacher,' said Dad, 'and besides, she'll know about all the nonsense soon enough, and she'll be sick of it sooner still. Meanwhile, I propose we let her stay innocent for the time being.'

He spoke in his I-don't-want-to-discuss-this-any-more tone of voice. Mum let the subject drop and I never got to hear from him where all the bitterness came from.

Anyhow, after much discussion between themselves, and with me, Mum decided I would go to the Academy (and Dad agreed. That's how it happens in our house; she decides, he agrees). She had two reasons; one, the school had a strong art department, and two, it had a good choir. They'd been to sing in York and Brussels. Mum made the right decision about the school because that's where the rest of the gang decided to go as well.

My room was then done up as my reward for passing the Transfer Test. The walls were painted yellow. The doors and windows were painted white. Mum bought an old wardrobe in town and painted it blue. She bought a red rug for the floor and a pine table with a chair for the corner. Dad put up a half cupboard with glass doors and I put all my glass animals on the shelves. The old curtains were replaced with muslin curtains.

We also agreed that the Spiderman duvet cover,

which I'd had since I was five, wouldn't do anymore. One Saturday afternoon, we went up to Belfast, to Mark's & Spencer's, just the two of us. I chose a new duvet cover. It was blue with yellow flowers all over it.

We bought some other things and then we went to a café. Mum ordered a cup of coffee from the woman behind the counter. I spotted some cartons of Five Alive in the cooler. Mum didn't allow this drink; it was pure sugar, she said. But perhaps today, I thought, because it was a special day, she'd let me have it. But then I asked myself, did I really want one? And the answer that came back was no, I didn't. What I really wanted was a cup of tea. I suppose I was losing my sweet tooth.

There was only the one free table and it was dirty. Mum got a J-Cloth from behind the counter to wipe the table. I wished she could have just sat at the table as it was. The ash and that on it didn't bother me and I felt uncomfortable with everyone staring at us as she busied herself. Mum, naturally, noticed nothing.

At last we sat down; Mum with her coffee, me with my tea. Mum squeezed my hand suddenly. I wanted to take my hand away from her hand but I didn't. It would have hurt her.

'You're really growing up so fast,' she said.

Then she pulled the duvet cover out of the bag.

'Isn't it nice?' she said.

There were tears in her eyes.

PART TWO
My Wish was a Boyfriend

1 A wish

I woke up but I lay still.

It was coming up to the end of small school. There were two months of holidays and then I started big school.

An hour later I stepped out of the house, no Tom at my side; this morning he had a sore throat and a sniffle and Mum was letting him stay home for the day. I think he wanted her attention and he had exaggerated his symptoms. But I was delighted. It was nice to be free of him.

It was a lovely still, May morning. The sun was already high, and the ground was already warm. I walked down our track. I kicked at the dirt. A small cloud of yellow dust rose around my feet. It hadn't rained for a week. When I got to the bridge, I stopped and looked over the side. The river was just a trickle.

I went on to the bottom of the lane and sat down on the bench Dad had put there for Tom and me to sit on when we waited for the bus.

I looked along the road. There was no sign of the bus. I looked at my watch. It was ten past eight. The bus was late.

I put my hand under the bench and found the small pile of stones which I had prepared. I selected three round heavy stones and dropped them between my legs. They were caught by my skirt.

I looked across the road to the lane that led up to Mrs Milligan, our opposite neighbour's house. There was a sign on the corner of the road and the lane. It read, *Drymen House. Bed & Breakfast.* The sign was attached to a metal pole, which was directly opposite me.

I stared at the pole. Its black shadow lay across the road. The tarmac was already warm from the sun and I could smell it.

My intention was to throw three stones at the pole, just as I had done every morning since the boy thing started. If I hit it three times (which so far I had not managed) I would get my wish. I had made only one condition. I was not allowed to stand.

I squinted across at the pole again and weighed a stone in the palm of my right hand.

My wish was a boyfriend. I didn't even have to think about it.

Now where did this come from? Why did I wish for this rather than anything else?

The answer is, I simply don't know. It was just something that had come some days earlier. I was getting on with Emma and the others fine, and they weren't talking about boys any more than they usually did. All I know is it just suddenly happened to me. I wanted a boyfriend the way you suddenly get a craving for something.

And so now here I was, on the bench, with three stones which I had taken from my store, about to try my luck. But before I went I said the word to myself. Just saying the word boyfriend to myself made me squirm on the bench with pleasure. Then I imagined a boy, not a real boy but a boy like I might have seen in a comic, and I squirmed again. One day I didn't think about boys, and then the next day I did.

I weighed the stone again and closed my left eye. Because I was sitting down it was easier to throw underarm than overarm.

I dropped my arm down on the far side of the arm-rest and towards the ground. The grass grew high here and I felt the sharp points of the grass needling my knuckles.

My wish was a boyfriend.

I raised my arm and exhaled. I opened my palm. The stone flew out of my hand. I watched the stone arc across the road. The stone hit the metal pole. There was a faint metallic ping.

I took a second stone and dropped my arm down over the side of the bench.

My heart was beating.

My wish was a boyfriend.

I tried to imagine that an invisible string connected the stone in my hand to the pole on the other side of the road.

My heart was beating faster. If I went on thinking like this I would not be able to throw properly.

I imagined there was a hole in the stone, and the invisible string was threaded through the hole, and that when I released the stone, it was going to shoot along the string to the pole . . .

I brought my arm up. I opened my fingers. The stone flew out. I knew it was another perfect throw. Then there was a faint ping. The stone bounced off the pole and landed by a clump of nettles.

I had had two hits. One more and my wish was going to come true.

My heart raced faster.

I had often scored two hits but I had never scored three hits.

I had never scored three hits because I got nervous.

'I must not be nervous,' I said to myself. 'I must not be nervous.'

I took the third stone. I had reserved the roundest and heaviest for last.

I dropped my arm. The grass brushed my knuckles. I noticed a new rabbit hole in the bank behind the pole.

My arm rose but I hadn't told it to rise.

My palm opened but I hadn't told it to open.

The stone flew out of my palm. I watched the stone fly across the black road.

Ping! I heard.

My eye was still on the road where the shadow of the stone had been.

I lifted my eyes. I saw the stone flying back from the pole. It sailed through the air and landed near the rabbit hole in the bank at the end of Mrs Milligan's garden. A rabbit ran out, brown with fawn ears and feet.

My wish would surely come true.

The rabbit sniffed the stone. His whiskers trembled. I heard a rumble in the distance and looked along the road. The yellow bus was coming.

I stood up and lifted my school bag on to my shoulder.

The rabbit looked across the road at me. His eyes were dark and alert.

My wish was going to come true. I had hit the pole three times in a row.

The rabbit bolted back into his hole.

The bus pulled up and the door hissed open.

I climbed the steps and looked down the aisle of the bus. I was looking for somewhere to sit. Nicola wasn't there. Her parents had taken her to Lanzarote for a week's early holiday, lucky beggar.

I saw faces staring back at me. I recognised some but most I didn't recognise. The children I didn't know were from another run who'd been put on to our run.

I felt my face and my ears reddening. The door banged shut behind me.

I noticed there were several free seats towards the back but I didn't fancy walking down there with everyone staring at me. Someone was going to make a crack about my red face. I saw an empty seat a couple of rows back. I decided to take it.

I hurried over and plonked myself down. The girl by the window went, 'Sorry.'

Her rucksack was beside her, wedged between us. I lent outwards and she pulled it out of the way. I shoved myself down the seat. I didn't get far. She was a plump girl; took up more than half the seat. Now I was uncomfortable. Perhaps I should go to the back, after all? As I thought about this, the bus turned and slowed. I was vaguely aware of jeering and then a chant starting up in the rear. Two or three voices, then a couple more; no more than half-a-dozen. But though the voices were few, they were loud and boisterous and there was an edge to them. I felt nervous. There was something about this shouting that I didn't like. I looked at the girl beside me.

'What are they saying?' I asked.

The girl turned away and looked out through the

window. She didn't want to speak. This shouting was connected to something embarrassing or unpleasant, and she definitely wasn't going to tell me what it was.

I sensed the bus slowing down further. We were coming into Crookedstone. In the distance I saw a cordon of white tape and a building behind with scorch marks up the front, and I knew then what the shouting was about – Lufty's hardware shop.

Dad had covered the story for the paper. He told me that two firebombs were left in Lufty's wood store on Saturday afternoon. The fire started at midnight. Fire engines were called out but they couldn't save any stock.

Dad went over on Sunday afternoon to have a look. He said the plastic handles on all the tools had melted, all the cans of paint had exploded, and the nails which Mr Lufty sold had fused together into big lumps.

The shouting was getting louder and more excited now. I turned in my seat. Several older boys I didn't recognise were standing and pointing at Lufty's.

I could understand them now. My ear had adjusted. 'One-nil,' they were shouting, and then roaring with laughter, and swinging their arms in the air as if they were holding football scarves and their team had just scored a sensational goal. They were happy but they were also angry in a way that reminded me of the ferry and the Orangemen.

The indicator clicked. The children in the back stamped their feet and applauded. First, it had only been a few voices; but now, judging by the decibel level, everyone at the back had joined in; the girls down there were with the boys.

At the same time as the noise got louder, I could feel the girl beside me wriggling on the seat. She was embarrassed and fearful at the same time. And I could see the same mixture of feelings on the faces of some of the children sitting near me. They looked frightened and appalled. And I could see that they were thinking like I was thinking. Get off, that was the thing to do. But if you got off, what did you do then? You'd be stuck in Crookedstone. If I got off, I'd have to call home, I thought. And what would Mum say? 'Phoebe, you're a very silly girl. What on earth did you get off the bus for?'

The bus pulled up at the bus stop and stopped. I wasn't going to get off, I realised. And I saw no one else was, either. The shell of Lufty's shop was only a few feet away. It was an old grey building, four storeys high. Sheets of new plywood filled each window. The plastic sign over the front door had melted and dripped down like wax. There was a policeman standing underneath holding a machine gun and looking blankly at the bus. I'd seen a couple of other places which had been bombed or fire bombed since we came to Northern

Ireland, so I wasn't surprised by what I saw.

Now someone shouted, 'Lufty faces relegation but the IRA goes through to the final.'

Several children on the bus started clapping their hands. Then the chant started again, louder than ever, jubilant and ugly, 'One-nil, one-nil, one-nil . . .' I thought, I'll have to get out. I'll have to go and ring Mum. Then I saw the driver turning and standing and I realised he was going to say something. I felt relieved. I thought I might suddenly burst out laughing. Or crying.

'Hey!' the driver shouted in the direction of the back of the bus, 'would you cut that out!'

But the children were oblivious; they knew they could pretend they hadn't heard, and they went right on chanting, 'One-nil, one-nil, one-nil.'

'Shut up,' the driver shouted at the top of his voice. It was so very loud that now the children couldn't go on pretending any more that they couldn't hear him. The chanting stopped and there was a horrid silence instead.

'Mr Lufty lost his business. You ought to be ashamed of yourselves, gloating like that,' the driver continued, at the top of his voice. He shook with anger. He was frightening too. 'And someone might have been killed. It's lucky no one was.'

'He was an Orange git and he got what he deserved,' a voice shouted back from the end.

There was another silence; this was much worse than the last.

Then, outside the bus, someone shouted from the pavement, 'Come on, open the door will you?'

This was one of the children waiting at the bus stop. There was a clunk, dull, metallic, as the caller tugged on the handle, hoping to open the door.

The bus driver waved at the children outside, indicating they should wait. 'You all ought to be ashamed of yourselves,' he continued, coldly furious more than angry now, 'and as for the last speaker, that was a disgusting remark. Mr Lufty did not deserve what happened. He's just a man trying to make a living.'

'Orange jerk, you mean.'

I saw the driver shake his head slowly. His face stopped being furious and became very hard, very ugly. I saw him close his fists. I could see what he wanted to do. He wanted to go down to the back. He wanted to hit. He wanted to fight. I felt my stomach shrinking. I tried to imagine what it was like, in the middle of me. I imagined a ball of cling-film, closed in on itself, wrinkled and hard, and impossible to ever open out again into a flat sheet.

At that, the very lowest, the very worst moment, someone outside shouted impatiently, 'Come on, will ya open the door, mister?' and rapped with a coin on the window right beside me. The noise was so loud and so sudden, it was like a gun shot and it made everyone on the bus jump out of their skins, even the driver, I think. Now his face changed again. The terrible hardness drained away and he looked more like he did when he first got up to speak, and at the same time he turned and looked at the boy in the road outside.

'Open the door, please,' the boy called through the glass, politely. He was about twelve years old, ironed shirt and a tightly-knotted tie. This twelve-year-old had no idea what was happening on the bus, only that the door was locked and he wanted to get on.

'Please, Mr Driver, sir,' the boy continued, and he put his hands together as if he was praying.

The girl beside me laughed. She would have laughed at anything, I know, no matter what it was. One or two other girls laughed with her. The laughter of the girls was nervous and strained but it filled the awful silence and it gave everyone something to copy. So very soon everyone was laughing in a fake way, the whole bus, and the boy outside could see that everyone inside was laughing, and knowing he was producing an effect, he got down on his knees and put his hands up to the sky, and now everyone crowded around the windows saw what was happening, and the sound of genuine laughter filled the air.

The bus driver turned and, shaking his head, he walked back to the front. Still shaking his head, he pressed the button and the door opened.

A load of children clambered up the steps and ran towards the back and the free seats. The last ones had to take the few remaining seats at the front.

I watched someone sitting down in the seat behind the driver – which is possibly the least popular seat on the bus – and then I noticed there was someone already in that seat. He looked incredibly familiar, with his black hair cut very, very short from the neck to about half-way up the back of his head. But where did I know him from? It was just like having a tune on the tip of my tongue and not being able to sing it.

We entered town and the bus pulled up at the first stop, St. Malachi's, the Catholic boys' secondary school. The boy stood up and turned to reach his bag from the shelf above. I saw his face and of course now I knew who it was. It was John Leary. His home was down the road and he got on before me. John was a first year at St. Malachi's. His father, Michael, had rescued Fred from the road and brought him home on his tractor on our first day. Since then, Dad had got Michael to do some things for us which needed special tools, like cutting our hedges and cleaning our drains. Anyhow, seeing John today, in his uniform, I thought how nice he looked. Then I remembered the third stone pinging on the pole and my face went red.

John noticed I was looking at him. He turned to

look back at me. A line of St. Malachi's boys were squeezing past him, and hurrying towards the steps, shouting and pushing one another.

John's arm came up and I saw the flat of his palm. I lifted my arm and waved back at him. He smiled. His teeth were white and lovely and straight. Any moment he was going to turn, I thought, and chase down the aisle with the other boys.

The seconds ticked on and soon our smiles felt forced. At last John turned away. My face went down like a burst paper bag.

John bent towards the driver. I felt relieved. He put his hand on the driver's shoulder. John had a strong forehead, the hair swept back from it, and a strong profile. I saw his mouth start to move. The driver smiled. John pointed at the back of the bus. The driver smiled again, put his hand on John's hand and squeezed. John was apologising for what had happened earlier. He had to be.

Then he straightened up. Now I knew he'd been waiting to say sorry to the driver, rather than to speak to me, I felt hurt.

I shan't smile at him when he goes, I decided. I was going to stare intently at the sign on the side of the road that said Control Zone. But John caught my eyes and before I could look away he was waving again and smiling and shouting, 'Hiya, Phoebe.'

Then he turned and ran down the steps, the door huffed and the bus moved off again.

'You a friend of John Leary?' asked the girl beside me in a thin, reedy voice.

'Yes,' I said, in my neutral tone of voice.

'You lucky beggar! I think he's dead gorgeous, so he is!' she said, while at the same time making a real effort to slide down the seat and make more room for me.

'Dead gorgeous,' she said, and I felt myself quivering all over.

2 Happiness together

At school, at break time, I was in the yard with the gang.

I said, 'There was cheering on the bus this morning.'

'Cheering you, were they, Phoebe?' said Emma quickly. 'I should ride on your bus with you one morning and see what goes on.'

Emma's house was on a different road to ours, and therefore was served by a different bus to mine. But actually, even if we had lived on the same road, I doubt we'd have seen each other on the bus very often. Emma liked her sleep, liked to get up as late as possible. She almost always missed her bus and I'd say Linda had to bring her in almost every morning.

'No, no one cheered me,' I said. 'The cheering was for Lufty's shop.'

'That would be the St. Malachi's crowd,' said Emma. 'That would be about their level. The whole school came out during the hunger strike, so they did.'

'Not at all. Not at all.' This was Sarah speaking. She had a bag of crisps in one hand and a crisp in the other which she held up to the sky.

'What are you doing?' demanded Emma.

'This crisp is almost perfectly round, and in the middle it's got an almost perfectly round hole, and I'm looking through the hole at the sky.'

'So it is,' I said. It was perfectly round, just a bit bigger than a fifty pence piece.

'And no, they didn't come out,' continued Sarah.

'Oh yeah?' Emma sounded peeved. She didn't like to be contradicted. She liked to be the authority. She liked to have the last word. 'Says who?'

'My aunt. She's a cleaner at St. Malachi's. All that happened was a few boys came out one lunch time and sat down in the road for ten minutes. It was more for the sheer hell of it than anything else and the whole thing was blown out of proportion.'

She was still staring in wonder at her crisp.

'If we sent this to Tayto crisps, the world's first perfectly circular crisp, do you reckon they'd give us money?'

'In your dreams.' Emma snatched the crisp from Sarah and put it straight in her mouth.

'That was a perfectly round crisp!' shouted Sarah angrily.

'I've eaten it. Give us another.'

Sarah's brown eyes went very black and her little body went very stiff.

Emma flashed her really charming smile. 'Go on,' she said, 'I could really murder another crisp.'

Emma stood there and smiled, with her hand out, daring Sarah to be petty, to turn around and stamp away with her crisps. To do that would be to cut herself off from us, and more especially from Emma, for the break, perhaps for the rest of the day. To do that would also be to show that she was childish, and spoilt, and couldn't take a joke. Would Sarah turn and flounce? Or would she forget what had happened and stay? I noticed Nicola watching. She had puffed up her cheeks, then by pressing outwards with her tongue she moved her moles from underneath.

'What are you doing?' asked Emma.

'Wriggling my moles.' Nicola kept her mouth shut so the words came out slurred. She sounded like a tape recorder when the battery is going flat. It was all that was needed to change the atmosphere.

'You're just silly, Nicola,' said Sarah, and she offered her crisps to Emma.

'Oh, thanks.' Emma smiled again. It was a lovely glorious smile, and suddenly we were happy again to be with each other.

'There was someone on the bus this morning,' I said. I did a little shimmy and beamed like a Cheshire cat.

'Oh yes. Superman, was it?' This was Emma. She

said this in a nice way, not a nasty way, encouraging me to go on.

'No, it was someone I rather fancy.'

'Ohhhhhh,' shouted Emma, Nicola and Sarah with one voice. 'Ohhhhhh.'

They closed around me in a circle.

'Tell us more,' said Nicola.

Sarah said, 'Who d'ya fancy?' and the three started laughing. Their laughter was nervous; at the same time it was like a laugh on the Big Dipper; it was all out of control.

'Well, who?' asked Nicola again. Her eyes shone like black olives. She spoke the least of us but sometimes I wondered if she thought the most.

'John,' I said.

'John what?' said Emma.

'You know the Learys?' I said.

Emma nodded.

'Well, John.'

'Oh him,' Emma said, 'John Leary.'

'Who's he?' asked Sarah.

I explained where the Leary farm was. They had all been out to my house, so they knew vaguely what I was talking about. John, on the other hand, was a blank. I said he looked a bit like Darlene's boyfriend in 'Roseanne'.

'That's right,' said Emma. 'He does look a bit

like Darlene's boyfriend, only he's cuter.'

The bell rang and I followed my friends across the playground with a warm glow inside. Emma, who was not normally given to paying compliments, had just paid me a huge one.

Mum took us into town after school. One of the High Street shops had free make-up that afternoon. We all got some on and then crammed into the photo booth in the Diamond in the centre of the town, and got our picture taken. We all looked quite daft.

Then my mum took us all home. The day was warm and to escape from the boys we went for a walk. First we went along the track at the back of the house, then we branched off the track, and went along a concrete lane which leads up to an abandoned house on the top of a hill. Suddenly, we saw soldiers running across the field beside us. They ran into the abandoned house. They looked very agitated and excited. There was a helicopter overhead. It hovered very low.

'Let's go and see what's happening,' shouted Emma.

I could see the green uniforms of the soldiers through the gaping windows of the abandoned house as I ran after her.

'I hope they catch someone and then we can go on the six o'clock news and say we saw it,' Nicola shouted.

'And we've got our faces on,' shouted Sarah.

As we came to the abandoned house, the soldiers

were filing out. They moved very quickly and they didn't look us in the eye. They circled the house and began to walk away past some old farm buildings.

'It's all right, Gerry,' Emma shouted suddenly, which was very bold.

'Yes, you can come out now, Gerry Adams,' Sarah called. She added the surname so the soldiers knew we meant the leader of Sinn Fein. We thought it hilarious to shout his name near the soldiers.

'Gerry, they've gone,' called Nicola.

'Come on, Gerry,' I added. I didn't want to be left out, so the gang could turn round later and accuse me of not joining in the fun.

'Gerry, Gerry, Gerry,' we all chorused then.

The soldiers had not responded, but now the one at the back of the line couldn't stop himself. He turned round. His eyes were very white in the middle of his boot-polish covered face. I think he smiled but it was difficult to tell. He waggled a finger then and that really cracked us up. The laughter doubled us up and went on so long my sides began to hurt.

After a while we all stopped; then Nicola cried, 'Gerry!' and we all started again, and that stopping and starting happened three or four more times, until finally we all felt there really wasn't any more laughter left in us.

It was very quiet. The helicopter was gone. The

soldiers were gone. We went up and peered into the abandoned house. There was sheep wool caught on the sharp edge of a stone. It was cream-coloured and very oily.

'Gerry!' shouted Sarah suddenly. The laughter started again, and it went on and on, until finally Emma shouted, 'This has got to stop. It hurts.'

'Yes, it has to stop,' I said, 'the laughing has to stop. It hurts.'

It felt as if the four of us had joined to form one person. What one thought, everyone thought. It was the greatest feeling ever. I was joined to Nicola and Sarah, and we three were joined to Emma, who was in the middle of this composite person.

I didn't have Emma's strength of personality, I didn't have her style. None of us did. It was right that she should be the sun, and that we were the planets that revolved around her.

We turned and walked down the lane and towards the track that would lead us back to my house. We linked arms and we began to sing, the four of us. We sang 'Amazing Grace'. Our voices were sweet and pure, and as we walked I imagined I was in the air looking down on us below. I saw the four of us in our dark school uniforms on the concrete lane that was the colour of butter. I heard our sure voices as they drifted across the fields on either side of the lane, fields that were filled with lush grass and flowers. I saw the shadows of the trees as they lay on the ground.

I was happy at that moment as I had never been happy before in all my life. In the bright sunlit morning, I had hit the metal pole at the end of Mrs Milligan's lane with a stone three times and who was to say what would happen in the months to come, and whether I would bump into John Leary again. Meanwhile, however, on a warm May evening, I had sung at the top of my lungs with my friends. I knew this was a day that I was never going to forget.

3 Batman returns

Just before school broke up, I went out one night to the Erne Screen Scene with Linda and Emma to see 'Batman Returns'. We bought our tickets and then we queued at the confectionery place. I bought a Pepsi Max and large sweet popcorn and a Mars bar. Emma bought the same except she chose Minstrels instead of a Mars bar.

'That's disgusting,' said Linda, as we started to amble across the foyer. 'You are stuffing yourself with sugar. Where are you putting it all?'

'We're growing, you see, and we burn it off,' said Emma.

She was wearing a T-shirt and a long skirt. Emma could only wear both items because she was so thin. In a very irritating but also very typically Emma-like way, she now twirled in front of her mother. Her skirt floated up. For a second the skirt was an upside down flower turning on the floor, and her body sticking up above was the stalk.

'I'm a skinny malink and you wish you were a skinny malink,' said Emma. 'Nuh-nuh-nuh-nuh-nuh!'

She stuck her tongue out at her mother. 'You're just jealous because you're always saying you're going to diet, but you don't. You ain't got the will power, so you don't.'

I'd never spoken to my mum like this. Never. Nor would I. It made me feel uncomfortable, this banter. It was like they were best friends rather than mother and daughter. But I think I was also jealous as I listened to Emma and then watched her twirling. I wanted to be like her.

'Listen, girls, listen to the voice of experience here,' said Linda, in her loud bossy voice. You had to listen when she talked like this. We had reached the back of a short queue. 'Look at this, girls.' Linda patted her middle. She had on a big pullover and one of her big, loose dresses underneath. Linda dressed like this, with lots of layers, because she thought of herself as fat, and she hoped the layers would hide everything. Myself, I'd say she wasn't fat; myself, I'd say she was just plump.

'When you get to my age, you want to lose a pound, you go through agony; you want to lose a stone, you go through hell.'

There were murmurs of agreement from the people around us. Linda sensed this and was pleased.

'Make it easier for yourself later on. Don't get into the habit of eating that junk now.'

'Listen to your mother – she's right, and I should know!' said the man who took our tickets.

His stomach hung down over his belt and the fat on his chest wobbled under his white shirt. He had a small pointed beard and there was sweat all over his face. He was huge, a haystack.

Linda took back our torn tickets with a smile and, so he would hear, she said very loudly as we walked towards the cinema, 'Pay attention to what the man says, girls.'

Linda lifted her arms and puffed out her chest and her cheeks.

'Wibble-wobble,' mocked Emma.

We all laughed as we went down the cinema aisle and we were still laughing when we took our seats near the front.

We drove home after the cinema in Linda's car, talking about the film. It was a warm, moist night, sort of muggy.

The road to Crookedstone was narrow and bendy, high hedgerows on either side. Moths and flies showed up in the head lamps of the car. Then a faint red light appeared some way ahead of us, circling in the darkness.

'Alert, alert,' said Emma in her computer voice.

The brakes squealed and Linda pulled down her sun visor and felt along the back of it.

'Oh no,' said Linda, but without sounding in the slightest bit anxious.

'What?' asked Emma.

'I don't have my driving licence. It's on the hall table. I meant to bring it but I forgot. Silly me.'

'Well, you'll just have to flutter your lashes and smile, won't you?' said Emma. Then she added in a high-pitched voice, 'Oh silly me, I left my licence at home.'

We were closer to the light now and I saw it was held by a figure in a helmet. It was a soldier. He was now waving the light backwards and forwards. A sign 'Stop Checkpoint' showed in front of the head lamps. I could see other dark figures lurking in the ditch on either side of the road. Only the whites of their eyes showed in the middle of faces which were covered with boot polish. It was a Vehicle Checkpoint, called a VCP for short. The first one of these I went through just after we arrived had been a bit nerve-racking; well, it would be, to me, coming from London, to be stopped in the dark by men with guns who then shone their torches into my face. But I'd been through dozens, even hundreds since, and I'd got used to them. In fact, I'd got to the stage where I didn't even notice them.

Linda stopped and wound her window down.

The soldier with the light came forward. There were bits of branch stuck in the net on his helmet.

'Hello,' he said.

'I don't have any identification.' This was Linda and she said it quickly.

'Oh,' said the soldier.

'What is it?' a voice called from the darkness.

'No licence,' the soldier called back.

The first soldier disappeared and the voice appeared in the window.

'Do you have any identification?' he asked. His accent sounded local.

'No. I left it at home. I'm terribly sorry,' said Linda quietly. 'I don't even have my banker's card or anything. I just came out with my purse. We've been at the cinema.'

'Oh really. What'd'ya see?' he asked.

'Batman Returns.'

'I was thinking of going myself. How was it?'

'Not bad but there were one or two gruesome bits.'

'Not frightening at all,' said Emma.

'I disagree,' said Linda. 'What about when Cat-woman gets attacked by all the cats in the alley and then goes and wrecks her room and stabs her teddy bears. Ugh!' Linda shivered. 'I didn't like that at all.'

'Typical Catwoman behaviour,' said Emma, 'nothing scary about it.'

'Don't you like cats?' said the soldier. He addressed the question to Linda.

'Not really.'

'A dog person, are you?'

'Yes,' said Linda, 'I suppose I am a dog person really.'

'Except we don't have a dog,' chimed Emma.

'I'd be a dog person too,' said the soldier.

'Do you have a dog?' said Linda.

The pair of them started discussing different dogs and I stopped listening.

Emma touched my hand in the darkness. I put my ear to her mouth and she whispered, 'We could be here for hours.' She faced forward. 'Linda, can we have long Wave Radio Atlantic 252?' she asked, giving the full title of the pop station we both liked to listen to.

'Certainly not,' said Linda, 'I'm talking.'

A car pulled up behind us and the soldier motioned Linda to pull over to the side of the road. She pulled over and the soldier came over. He squatted down on his haunches bringing his face down to the same level as Linda and they went on talking. Bits of paper were passed in and out of the window. I guessed they were giving each other their telephone numbers.

'Could we please have Atlantic 252?' repeated Emma.

'Would you please be quiet, Emma, I'm talking to Arthur.'

'Do you want to know what I thought of the film?' said Emma.

Arthur laughed.

'No, he does not want to know,' said Linda humorously, 'now just talk among yourselves, girls.'

While the grown-ups talked, Emma and I sat silently, staring out of the window. I was on the same side as the road. I watched the Checkpoint, cars pulling up, drivers talking to the soldiers through their windows, drivers getting out, opening their boots, soldiers looking inside. There was one car full of people and the boot was full of luggage. The soldiers asked for the luggage to be opened. One of the women in the car shouted something at the soldiers but no one paid any attention. The driver opened the suitcases. I glimpsed shirts and dresses as the soldier rummaged around. Then the suitcases were closed up and the soldiers started lifting them back. Only the latches weren't properly closed on one and the lid fell open and everything tumbled out on to the ground.

'For God's sake!' shouted the driver.

Arthur, still babbling away to Linda at the window, glanced back over his shoulder and said, 'Oh dear.'

'Shouldn't you go over,' asked Linda, 'seeing as you're in charge?'

'They can sort it out,' said Arthur.

The soldiers were kneeling on the road, picking up the clothes and putting them back in the suitcase. They were trying to do it carefully but they were making a complete mess, and when it came to close the lid, the case was so badly packed it wouldn't shut.

'Oh never mind,' said the exasperated driver.

He lifted the bulging suitcase into his boot and slammed the lid down angrily.

'I'm very sorry,' said the soldier.

The driver got into his car and drove off.

Arthur and Linda went on talking. For hours it seemed. Eventually Linda said goodbye and we drove off.

'Right, girls,' she said, 'as of now, I, Linda Turtle, mother of one, shall be going on a diet.'

'Oh really?' asked Emma. 'I thought you were resigned to your size.'

'I was,' said Linda, 'but that was before Arthur asked me on a date.'

'And what about "Le Situation"?' said Emma. This was the term my dad had invented to describe Linda's romantic life. At that time she had two boyfriends – Ken, an architect's draughtsman, and Micky, a heating engineer. They were both very keen on Linda but she couldn't decide between the two of them, I think because she didn't like either of them all that much.

'Two timing,' continued Emma, who sounded like she was really enjoying herself, 'is bad enough, but three timing, Mother, is unacceptable.'

'Oh to hell with Ken and Micky,' said Linda

fiercely. 'I've finished with those two. I've got a better fish to fry now.'

4 John and Emma

It was the start of the holidays and I was having a swim. Suddenly, all the pool attendants were out and on the side of the pool, and they were all blowing their whistles and waving their arms frantically and shouting, 'Get out, get out.'

I got out. I was going to go down to the changing rooms for my towel, when one of the pool attendants stopped me and shouted, 'Where are you going?'

'To the changing room.'

'No, you're not! Out that way! Out the emergency exit! Now!' he shouted.

He pointed to the fire door.

'But I haven't got my towel,' I wailed.

'No towel, just out, now. There's a bomb scare, nothing to worry about. Just do as I say and go outside.'

I think if I'd been in one of these before, I wouldn't have been so daft as to want to go and get my towel. Of course, I'd heard about bombs but this was the first actual bomb scare I'd been in. Anyway, once I got the message, I acted quickly.

I went out the fire door and on to the fire escape

and then this cold breeze hit me. Instant goose pimples from head to toe. I started going down the steps. I was freezing, but worse was feeling all this dirt and grit and rust under my feet.

At the bottom of the steps another life guard pointed in the direction of the front of the building and we all went round.

The next bit was dead embarrassing, having to stand in my swimming costume at the front, firemen and policemen and soldiers and that pulling up and thundering past and running into the building. The swimming-pool attendants had a few silver blankets which they gave out to old people and mothers with babies. I didn't get one. But I did notice this boy had one. He was sitting on the edge of a rubbish bin with his back to me. As I looked at him, I felt dead resentful.

He must have felt my eyes boring into him, for the next thing, he turned around and looked right back at me, and I saw who it was. John Leary.

'Hello,' he said quietly.

He got up and came over and handed me the silver blanket.

'You look as though you need this more than me.'

My teeth were chattering. I took the foil blanket and pulled it tightly over my shoulders.

'It's freezing,' I said. It was freezing but at the same time I was blushing. I could hardly believe this was happening when I was so cold. Trust my face to let me down.

'I didn't recognise you before,' I said.

'Oh. I recognised you,' he said.

They looked like strong muscles on his arms.

'My mum's coming to get me,' I said, for no reason at all.

'She doesn't have to come all the way in for you. My mum and dad'll be here in a few minutes. They could give you a lift home if you want.'

I thought my heart was going to dance.

'Yes,' I said, 'yes,' and that was when they gave us the all clear and we filed back inside.

I got myself dried and into my clothes quicker than I'd ever managed in my life before, ever. Then I dashed to the foyer and called Mum on the pay phone; I told her I was getting a lift home with John.

'Oh,' said Mum, 'that's good.'

Now sometimes Mum says, 'That's good,' for want of something to say; the words just fill a space. And then sometimes she says, 'That's good,' and the words are there to stand in for something huge. They're like the tip that tells you there's an iceberg lurking under-water. And when she said it now, on the phone, it was the second way.

'Why do you say that?' I was careful not to sound worried.

'I don't know whether the phone is the place to discuss this,' she said, which was typical.

Then I had a flash of inspiration. 'You think I see too much of Emma, don't you?'

'I think it's important to widen one's circle.'

'So you do, don't you?'

'I didn't say that but all right, I suppose I do.'

Why couldn't she just have come out with it? Then the pips went.

'See you later, sweetie,' she said.

I put down the phone. I could feel the damp from my wet hair seeping through to my shoulders. In the rush of getting to the phone, I hadn't dried it properly. Did I have time to run to the changing room and use the hair dryer? I wondered.

I was just about to run down when I heard Emma's voice behind me. Oh no. Why her, now? This was complicated enough without her.

'Hey! There you are,' she said, sprinting over from the double doors. 'Where've you been? I've been phoning you.'

Linda came after her. She had hardly eaten since 'Batman Returns'. Her face was smaller, tighter but I preferred her the way she was before. When her face was plumper, she looked softer and kinder.

'Coming for a swim?' This was Emma.

'I've just been,' I said.

'Oh, come on.'

'No.'

Emma's expression was one of complete amazement. 'Come back in, don't be a spoil sport,' she pressed.

'I can't,' I said.

'Yes you can. Come on. Don't say no like that.'

'I'm being collected in a minute.'

'Ring your mother and ask her to come later. Come on. Don't make me go in by myself. It'll be so boring. I'll just have to swim up and down.'

'Don't worry, Emma, you can join me,' said Linda brightly. Then she added, 'I'm a forty-lengths-a-session girl now.'

'Go on, Phoebe, ring home.'

I noticed John had come into the foyer. He was standing at the notice board, pretending to read a poster about a swimming gala.

'I can't. I'm getting a lift with someone else.'

'With who?'

I lifted my eyes and glanced in John's direction.

'With, umh . . .' I said.

Emma glanced back over her shoulder.

'With John what's-his-name?'

I nodded.

'Well, just tell him you can't come now,' she said in a low voice. 'Or I will if you want. I don't mind. I'll say you're very sorry but you didn't expect to bump into me, your best friend, and now you want to go back in and swim with me, your best friend, and we'll bring you home later.'

'No.'

'Yes.'

'Emma, this is getting tedious,' said Linda. 'Phoebe doesn't want to stay.'

'Yes, she does.'

The phrase changed everything. How could she say that *she* knew what I wanted to do while *I* didn't know what I wanted to do. I most certainly did know what I wanted to do. I had hit the pole with the stone three times, and now I wanted to get a lift with John's parents. And Mum was right. Time to widen my circle. Until this point I'd been polite and reasonable with Emma. Now I felt annoyed and I didn't see why I should bother hiding my feelings.

'I don't want to swim,' I said. 'I don't want to stay with you. I want to go with John.'

'But I'm your friend.'

I couldn't think what to say.

'Don't you want to be with me?'

'You're going to see her tonight, Emma,' Linda interjected, which was true. I was going to sleep over at Emma's that night. 'I think you should just drop this.'

I saw my opportunity. 'Yes,' I said, 'and then I'll tell you what happened. I'll have some news, for once.'

'And you don't want to come in with me, now, and swim?'

'No, she doesn't. I think she's made that very clear, Emma. She's got a date.'

The way Linda used the word date, it was like it was underlined a hundred times, and I started to blush. I went light red; then I went dark red; then I went deep beetroot. I wished the earth would open up and swallow me.

'I'm so sorry, I didn't mean to make you blush,' said Linda sweetly. She angled my body so that John couldn't see my face from the notice board.

'Emma, no more discussion. We're going in to the pool, Phoebe's going home,' said Linda.

'All right,' agreed Emma, affable now. She thought my blushing was a victory for her.

'Even your ears have gone red, Phoebe,' she whispered.

She lifted some of my wet hair over them.

'Come on, Emma, we can't hang around all day.' Linda propelled her daughter towards the counter. 'You may not know how to take a hint, but I do know that you know what a shove is.'

Linda put her money down on the counter. 'Two swims,' she said. As they hurried back past me towards the changing rooms, Linda whispered, 'I've had some luck in the love department myself since the cinema.'

And then they were gone. The woman behind the desk smiled at me. I rubbed my rolled up towel on my neck. I could feel the blood draining from my face, the blush subsiding, and not a second too soon, for the next moment John was at my side.

'I don't know where my parents have got to,' he said.

I smiled. I was trembling but I was delighted. I'd done the right thing. I had said no. I had to say no. I had to do what I wanted and not what Emma wanted me to do. If I'd given in and gone back in to swim, she'd have thought she could boss me around for ever.

5 John and Fred

We drove home, neither of us saying much. I kept thinking back to what happened in the foyer. I wondered if Emma would have cared if it had been someone else I had been going back with, rather than John? I wondered if she was jealous but I couldn't be certain. Then, when we pulled up in front of my house, Mum rushed out and invited John to stay for lunch. He looked at me first and then he looked at his mother to know if he could accept. I said nothing but Mrs Leary said, 'All right then, John, you might as well, go on.'

Mrs Leary didn't sound like she was pleased. My heart was beating. I desperately wanted him to come in and, at the same time, I would have been tremendously relieved if John had turned and said, 'I think I'll go home, if you don't mind.'

The television was on in the front room. Fred was lying on the sofa watching 'Dumbo the Elephant', so I said, 'Let's watch TV. It's "Dumbo the Elephant".'

'Yes,' said John. He was as relieved as I was.

After twenty minutes we were called in to lunch and everything started getting excruciating again. John picked up his knife and fork and then, because he was so nervous, he dropped them. The whole place went absolutely silent.

Mum offered John a bowl and said in the special voice she reserves for young guests, 'Would you like some avocado salad, John?'

John took the bowl from her but he made no move to put any salad on his plate. He just stared into the bowl.

'Is something the matter?' Mum asked, which I knew was exactly the wrong thing to say.

'What's avocado?' asked John.

My ears went red hot like coals. Every now and again, I had this really strong feeling that we didn't fit in here. We were different. And when I had this feeling, I didn't want to be like us any more; I wanted to be like everyone else, and this was one of those times. Why couldn't we just have had fish and chips? I wanted to shout at my mum. Why must we have lentils and kidney beans and avocados and all these strange things that nobody in Fermanagh was used to. Why couldn't we just blend in? Why did we have to stick out like a sore thumb?

'It's a vegetable,' said Mum.

'Actually, isn't it a fruit?' said Dad.

'That doesn't matter,' said Mum, 'the point is you have it in a salad, with onions and hard-boiled eggs in this case, and it's very delicious.'

'I'll try it,' said John, and he spooned a tiny portion on to his plate.

'That's it, be adventurous,' said Mum.

I'll scream, I thought. Why can't she just leave him alone and shut up.

My dad asked John a few farming questions and a slow stop-start conversation started. Then Tom threw a kidney bean at Fred hitting him on the cheek and Fred began to cry and Mum got angry. She told Tom he had no table manners and she told Fred that there was no need to whinge.

'It's just like being at home,' said John tactfully. He had two sisters and two brothers, he explained. But as they were all quite a bit older than he was, I couldn't imagine them throwing food at the dining table. Naturally, I didn't say this. I was amazed that he could think of anything to say. I had this great warm sense of relief. He wasn't going to embarrass me. It wasn't going to be terrible.

Meanwhile, unlike John, my family were still behaving badly. Tom was annoyed that Mum had ticked him off in front of John. If there's one thing Tom can't stand, it's criticism in front of an older boy or anybody that he wants to like him. So he kicked Fred under the table, and Fred, who can gush tears at the drop of a hat, started to sob; you'd have thought he'd broken a leg.

Mum ticked Tom off. One more naughty thing and he'd go to his room, she said. Then she rubbed Fred's leg and offered to kiss the place where he hurt. Then she told him not to cry any more. None of this made the slightest difference. Fred just went on howling. John made funny faces. Dad made funny noises. But these had no effect either. So Mum took Fred on to her lap and stroked his head and kissed his ears, and finally the sobbing stopped.

Then the meal was over. 'All right,' said Mum to Fred. 'Down you get. We have to clear up.'

She put Fred down and he immediately started crying again. At the same time he rubbed his eyes and sniffled.

'Oh Fred, please,' said Mum, ever so slightly grumpily, 'give it a rest, will you?'

With a cry Fred ran through to the hall and a few seconds later I thought I heard him running into the front room, to the television, and the door banging shut after him.

A little while later, Dad came in from the hall and said, 'Anyone seen Fred?'

'He's in the front room,' I said, sweeping a load of bread crumbs into the dustpan. (Why did my brothers always manage to put so much food on the floor?)

'No,' said Dad, 'he's not in the television room.'

'Have you looked outside? Have you been to the

swing? Have you looked in the outhouses?' said Mum.

'I've been everywhere,' said Dad, 'upstairs, down-stairs, and outside, and I can't find him anywhere.'

'He can't have gone,' said Mum, 'children don't just vanish.'

She hung a wet tea towel over the radiator and walked out through the door and into the front hall calling, 'Fred, Fred, where are you?'

Dad went out the back door and I heard him calling across the yard, 'Fred, Fred . . .'

I finished sweeping the floor. John put the orange juice and the butter in the fridge.

Mum came back into the kitchen, Tom following her, just as Dad came in the door from the yard.

'Can't see him anywhere,' said Dad.

'Nor can I,' said Mum. 'But he must be somewhere.'

'He might have gone down to the lake.'

'What did you say, Tom?' asked Mum very calmly.

'He might have gone down to the lake,' said Tom.

The lake was at the back of the house. It wasn't far. There was nothing down there except a wooden pier. It was old, half collapsed and we had been warned that under no circumstances were we ever to go out to the end of it or even step up on to it.

'He likes going down there. He goes down there a lot. When he's sad I know he goes and looks at the water,' continued Tom.

'Does he go on the pier?' asked Mum.

'I'm sure he'd like some of the wood from it to add to our base in the rhododendron bush,' said Tom cheerfully.

Mum let out a shriek and Dad said, 'My God!'

We ran as a pack out the door and across the yard, over the bank and down the narrow winding track to the lake. The water was dark and smooth, fringed with rushes around the edges. The rotting pier was there but there was no sign of Fred. We ran over to the pier anyway but it looked just the same to me as the last time I'd looked. I was sure Fred hadn't been here.

'That's where he likes to sit,' said Tom, and he pointed at an upside down bucket a few feet from the pier. 'He likes sitting there and looking at the water.'

'I'm going to pull that wretched thing down,' said Dad. 'I don't know why I never got round to it.'

'Let's make a plan,' said Mum. 'He hasn't necessarily come down here. He might have gone up to the road and walked off that way. After all, that's what he did last time he disappeared.'

We decided to split into two parties. Dad, John and I would search around the lake; Mum and Tom would go back to the house and drive the car down to the road and search there in both directions.

There was a narrow path around the lake. John and I went along it clockwise, and Dad went along it anti-clockwise. The path was very thin and I had to walk in front of John. I was glad of that. I was frightened and I felt sick and worse, there were tears in my eyes. This was turning out to be one of the worst days of my life. All I'd wanted was a nice talk with John.

The lake was very black and very still. There was no wind and the rushes, which grew up out of the water, were absolutely motionless, like pencils sticking up in the air. No dogs barked, no birds sang, and there were none of the sounds which usually fill the countryside. I knew it was quiet because something awful had happened.

I once saw a drowned man on a beach in Italy. Now, searching amongst the rushes, staring at the still, black water, calling, 'Fred, Fred where are you?' I could feel the picture of the drowned man coming into my mind. I tried to stop it but I couldn't keep it out. And then, with my mind's eye, I saw what I'd seen on the beach, all mixed up with a picture I'd made up of Fred's small body floating in the water, face down, dressed in his little blue shorts and his Spiderman T-shirt.

I also couldn't stop thinking about sitting down on the sofa before lunch, John and I on either side of Fred, watching the video without saying one word. That was my last hour with my brother, our last precious hour together, and what had I done? Sat stupidly on the sofa, absolutely tongue-tied and watched 'Dumbo the Elephant'. I wanted to hit myself. I wanted to scream and wail and tears did come to my eyes.

I met Dad half-way around the lake. He said, 'I haven't seen him, have you?'

I shook my head. If I opened my mouth I was certain to stammer and blub.

'No,' said John, 'Phoebe and I have been looking and we didn't see him. He's certainly not in the water where we were.'

To my ears it sounded as if John was some sort of official and he was giving a report. But then I thought, well how else is he meant to sound? He hasn't asked for this. He's just here, he's helping out, and he's managing brilliantly. I was glad he was there, but in another part of me I wished he was gone. Because something awful had happened, I wanted us to be just family.

'Let's double-check,' said Dad. He instructed us to take the part of the path he had already been along, and he said he'd take the section we'd done.

When we met on the far side, John said to Dad, 'Nothing, Mr Rodgers.'

'Nothing,' replied Dad, and then he added, 'Right, he's not here then, he can't have drowned. Let's go back to the house.'

We walked up the track calling, 'Fred, Fred . . .'

over the walls and into the fields and copses of trees on either side, but there was no reply.

Then we got to our yard and we searched the outhouses, the turf shed, the boiler room, the greenhouse, the garden shed, the kennel, the lumber room, and the rabbit hutch, but there was no sign of Fred.

We heard the car coming. Mum drove up. Her face was red and tear-stained. Tom sat quietly at her side.

'I drove three miles in both directions and stopped a couple of farmers on their tractors,' Mum said quickly, 'but there's no sign of him in either direction.'

'There was no sign of him down at the lake,' said Dad.

'I suppose we'll have to call the police, then.'

'Yes,' said Dad.

He put his arm around Mum. We moved towards the front door slowly.

'Excuse me, Mrs Rodgers,' I heard John saying timidly behind me as we went in, 'can I use your toilet?'

Couldn't he have waited? This was an emergency.

'Go up the stairs and along the landing. It's at the back.'

As John bounded up the stairs two at a time, Dad, Mum, Tom and I went into the study and huddled around the phone.

'Hello, Enniskillen police station, please. Hello, is that the police station?' said Dad. 'I'm ringing about my son, Fred, Fred Rodgers. We haven't seen him for several hours now, and we're starting to get a bit worried.'

There was a pause while he listened.

'Have you?' said Dad, suddenly sounding hopeful. Apparently, there was a child in the police station.

Another pause.

'No, our son is five,' said Dad, sounding sad again.

Dad kept saying 'Yes,' and 'I suppose so,' and 'I see what you mean.' Then he said, 'Crookedstone. We live in Crookedstone.'

'Hey! I've found him.' John was jumping down the stairs.

'What's that?' said Dad. 'Oh sorry, I'm so sorry. I think he may have turned up.'

'I've found him,' said John from the doorway.

'We've found him,' said Dad and put the phone down.

'What?' said Mum.

'Upstairs,' said John.

He was looking at me. He wanted me to be impressed. I didn't look back at him. I couldn't. I had a feeling like something very hot and hard and rigid was suddenly filling the space in the middle of my body. It was relief mixed up with huge excitement and it was so powerful and strong, I thought my legs would buckle and I was going to fall. Part of me hadn't wanted John here. But now suddenly, it turned out he might be the hero.

'He's upstairs,' said John again.

'What's he doing up there?' Mum shouted.

'Yes, what?' shouted Tom.

'How can he be up there, Mum's already looked up there?' I called.

'He's asleep.'

'Asleep?' we said.

'Yes.'

We followed John up the stairs and into Fred's bedroom.

'He's in the cot, right under the covers,' said John.

'But he *never* sleeps in there!' said Mum. 'He just has it in the room for some reason. As a fort, I think.'

We all moved forward together, like a blob. Mum lifted back the duvet and I saw Fred's body. His shoulders and head were hidden right under the pillow.

'The little wretch,' said Mum.

Fred was on his side, his legs were one on top of the other, they were thin like the rods of the banister outside on the landing. His chest was going quietly up and down.

'How did you know Fred was here?' asked Mum.

'I heard him coughing.'

'And to think we were chasing around the lake and all round the place,' said Dad. 'Goodness me! I'm taking down that jetty.'

Fred murmured and moved his feet. The little clasps on his sandals jingled faintly.

'Let him sleep,' said Mum tenderly. 'He obviously needs it. And if we wake him, he'll be in a foul mood for the rest of the afternoon.'

Ever so gently, she covered him over again. Then we all filed down the stairs. 'Every time we lose that Fred, it's the Leary family who bring him back. I hope this isn't going to become a habit,' said Dad.

I saw John smile shyly. He was really delighted with himself, but from his expression I could tell he wasn't one to crow or strut or show off. I liked that.

Then Mum said, 'After all that excitement, I think it's time for a Jaffa cake and a cup of tea, don't you?'

After tea, John and I sat down to play Monopoly. Tom came up and said he wanted to play. I said no, but John said Tom could play on his side. So they were a team against me.

We started to play. We each bought up the properties we landed on, but neither of us were able to get a set and start building hotels. I think that's what happens when there are only two players, but I didn't mind. I was just happy to play.

Then I heard a car draw up outside, and a horn went toot-toot.

'That'll be my mother,' said John, 'I'd better go.

But I want to give you something,' he went on. He unfastened his leather necklace with the tiny leaping dolphin hanging on it. The figure was silver with a tiny jewel for an eye. He'd shown it to me earlier when I'd shown him my collection of glass animals with my dolphin in pride of place.

'But that's precious to you!'

He extended his arm towards me. The dolphin and the leather necklace lay in the palm of his hand. I wanted to snatch it up but the very fact of wanting it so badly made me think it must be wrong to take it.

'Oh, but I couldn't.'

The horn tooted again outside.

'There she is again. My mother. Go on. Take it.'

I took it and he smiled. I fastened the necklace at the back and smoothed the dolphin down on my front.

'I've got to go out to my mother now, or she'll kill me.'

After John had gone, I ran up the stairs and then back down the stairs, I ran out to the garden and back in to the kitchen, then I ran back to the garden and over to the swing. The dolphin hanging round my neck had been his and now it was mine!

I got on to the swing and began to swing up and down. I felt the air on my face. I felt the air ballooning my skirt. Every time I jerked forward the dolphin would swing forward and then smack back against me. It was a light thing but I could feel it. It was there, all right. John must be my boyfriend now.

I remembered how the third stone hit Mrs Milligan's signpost. Then how Emma'd nearly spoilt everything. But I'd managed to stop her doing that. And wasn't it wonderful that I had? I wouldn't have known this moment of pure bliss otherwise, on the swing, the air rushing past my face, my hair trailing behind, the small dolphin around my neck, swinging out and back as I rose and fell.

6 The phone call

'Let's see it,' said Emma.

I was in Emma's bedroom. It was that evening. I'd told her what had happened. She was in her bed. I was in the other bed. Now she wanted to see the necklace.

'What sort of stone is it?' she asked. She weighed it in the palm of her hand.

'I don't know.'

'I'm sure it isn't precious, whatever it is!' and she threw the necklace disdainfully back to me.

'How do you know?' I didn't let it show that she'd annoyed me.

'Because of the cheap, stupid leather thong.'

'It's not stupid,' I said. I thought the leather was brilliant. It smelt faintly of John.

'If the stone was precious it'd be on a chain, obviously.'

'John's a boy, maybe he didn't want to wear a chain.'

'Oh, he thinks chains are only for girls. He probably is backward in that way.'

There was resentment in her voice.

'Do you know how irritating you are?' I said.

'Tell me about it.'

'You're just jealous, because ever since I mentioned this necklace it's been dig, dig, dig.'

She blinked furiously and I knew I'd hit home. But being Emma, she tried to brazen it out.

'I'm trying to help you because you don't know how ridiculous this is. It's just a necklace but in your eyes it's this big thing which it's not.'

I fastened the leather necklace at the back. The flat metal of the dolphin was cold on my skin.

I heard a car pull up outside. I heard the sound of a man's voice.

'Oh great!' said Emma. I could tell she was relieved to change the subject. 'Do you know who that is?'

'No.'

'Guess.'

'I give up.'

'It's Arthur. You know, from the Checkpoint. "Are you a doggie person? I'm a sort of doggie person myself." '

Then in her normal voice she said, 'He's taken to sleeping over. He's got the hots for Linda.'

She lay back on the pillow, closed her eyes, opened her mouth, and began to pant. 'Ah-hah. Ah-hah. Ah-hah.'

I knew the sound of course. On television it was

embarrassing, and if I ever thought I was in danger of hearing it coming from my mum and dad's bedroom, I ran away. But in Emma's room it was funny.

I started to laugh.

'Can we have a bit of quiet up there, girls,' Linda called from downstairs.

'Sorry, Linda,' Emma shouted down in her best behaviour voice.

'Go to sleep.'

'Yes, at once, Linda.'

We laughed together.

'Let's stay awake,' said Emma, 'and listen to Linda and Arthur.'

We talked quietly as we didn't want Linda to know we were awake. We got on to the subject of glasses. Miss Ferguson, our teacher, had a new pair.

'I'd like glasses,' I said suddenly. 'I'd look more serious and I'd get served more quickly in a shop in glasses.'

Emma didn't say anything. The room was quiet except for the sound of our breathing and the bubbles in the fish tank.

'Emma?'

No reply. Emma never fell fast asleep. Perhaps she was just pretending? But I went to check and she was asleep. I thought, *we* were going to stay awake. And I didn't want to hear those noises, not without Emma, not on my own. I fretted about this for a while, with the bubbles from the tank fizzing in the darkness. Next thing, it was morning.

'Good morning!' I shouted across at her.

'What is it?' said Emma sleepily.

'You missed some fireworks last night,' I lied. 'By the way, I thought you were staying awake with me. Why did you fall asleep?'

'I didn't fall asleep, did I?' she said.

'Yes you did, chicken, chicken, chicken,' I chanted.

'Oh, shut up.'

'Chicken, chicken. Sick on you, fell asleep, chicken, chicken.'

'Don't be so childish,' said Emma tartly. She sat up in bed. 'Well?' she demanded. 'Tell me what happened?'

I decided to calm her down, to make light of everything. 'It was no big deal.'

'No big deal?'

'No,' I said, 'they just went – ah-hah, ah-hah – a couple of times and then . . .' and with that I closed my eyes and let out a long drawn out snore.

'Was that Arthur?' she asked.

'I don't know.'

'You must know. Linda's snore is more like a sigh. His is the piggy snore. Was it like a pig?'

'I don't know.'

'You're not very observant.'

That was Emma all over. Any chance to score a point, she just couldn't resist.

'Want to know the truth?' I said.

'All right.'

I had enjoyed feeling superior, but I knew better than to relish this for more than a moment.

'I fell asleep myself,' I said. 'I heard nothing.'

Her pillow came flying towards me. I put my arm up and caught it.

'You little minx, you fibber,' she laughed.

I'd done the right thing. Now there was going to be no surliness at breakfast.

I went to the bathroom to brush my teeth. As I stared at my face in the mirror, I started to think about John, comparing him with her. Emma kept me on my toes. She wasn't always nice but she was certainly always surprising. John seemed altogether the reverse. Maybe I liked him just because he was a change from her.

But how were things going to turn out, given she definitely didn't like the idea of him? The digs about the necklace had told me this, but even without them, I could have guessed. Emma was a control freak. She didn't like new people coming in and upsetting established relationships, particularly if she thought they were going to undermine her influence.

Ten minutes later, I went down the narrow steep stairs to the living room. There were old ashes from the night before in the grate and the curtains were closed. Arthur was whistling in the kitchen. I went through. I hadn't seen the man since the night at the Checkpoint. He looked much smaller without his uniform and his metal hat.

'I've heard a great deal about you,' he exclaimed, 'and all of it favourable.'

What could I say?

He said, 'I'm going to fry some tomatoes and have them on toast. Will you join me?'

I wrinkled my nose and made a noise. I hate tomatoes, I always have.

'I love them,' said Arthur.

'They're slimy,' I said as he slid the pan under the grill.

Emma bounded in, smelling of toothpaste.

'Oh, goody, my favourite,' she said.

Then she looked up at Arthur and said, 'Those tomatoes are for me, aren't they?'

'Be useful for once and bring this up to your mother.'

Arthur pressed a mug of tea into Emma's hand.

'And in return, I'll give you breakfast,' he said.

*

We were in the garden on the deck chairs under the apple tree. Arthur and Linda were out.

'If you don't ring John, then I'm going to ring him,' said Emma.

Now I didn't like this idea. Not a bit. My life was my business, not hers. It was a mistake to let her get involved, and it was a bigger mistake to let her start organising it. So I said, 'I don't want to ring him.'

'If you don't ring him, I'm going to ring him,' she said threateningly.

She circled John's family number in the directory with a purple Biro and drew a heart in the margin beside it.

'I don't want to ring him.'

'Yes, you do,' she said. She wrote Phoebe R and John L and added an arrow to the heart.

I decided to stall. 'What am I going to say?'

'Oh, easy. "Hello, this is Phoebe. Do you want to go out with me?" '

'I can't.'

I felt my face going red just at the thought of the words.

'You have to ask him.'

'I can't.'

'You have to. You haven't agreed anything yet. You're not "going out". Besides which, you've only the one life. The opportunity is here. Don't let it slip through your fingers.'

'I can't. I can't.'

'All right, suit yourself, but I shan't let you throw your life away.'

Emma let out a large sigh and slowly lifted herself out of the deck chair. 'The things I have to do for my friends,' she said.

'Give me that telephone book,' I shouted, but she skipped sideways before I was able to grab it off her.

'Give it back this instant.'

She ran across the grass and went in through the French doors, then pulled the bolt across inside.

'Emma,' I shouted, tugging the handle. 'Open these doors.'

'Nah,' she shouted through the glass.

'Open this door at once.'

'After I ring him.'

I began to sprint along the patio. If I could get in through the kitchen door I could stop Emma. But when I got round to the end of the building I saw Emma's face on the other side of the glass in the kitchen door. She was smirking. I tried the handle. It was locked. She showed me the key to the door through the glass.

'Are you going to ring him or do you want me to do it?' she shouted.

I had to get in. I had to stop her.

'I don't know,' I said calmly. 'I don't know if I'm ready yet. I might not be ready. A relationship is a serious matter. It's not just for Christmas, you know.'

'What? What are you on about?'

'I was thinking about the ad, you know, "A puppy is for life, not just for Christmas." '

'What's that got to do with anything?'

'I don't know.'

'You're completely daft,' she said.

'I probably am.'

I moved away from the door and lazily stretched my arms towards the sky as if I hadn't a care in the world. Only the front door remained open. I would have to get in that way and stop her.

Suddenly, I set off. I ran round the house at a tremendous lick. Yes, I was going to do it.

But when I got within a couple of paces of the door, I saw Emma was already in the porch. She madly swung the door shut, and as it swung, it pushed out the round stone that Linda used as a door stop.

The door slammed, the latch clicked, the heavy round stone bumped over my feet and ploughed into the gravel.

'Ouch!' I shouted as if I was in terrible pain which I wasn't. 'You've broken my ankle with the stone.'

'Don't be such a baby,' shouted Emma.

'Ouch! You have. Let me in.'

I hammered frantically on the wood. 'I can't walk,' I shouted.

The brass letter flap flipped up and Emma's blue eyes stared out.

'What are you talking about, you look perfectly fine.'

I staggered as if my ankle was gone and screamed in agony.

'It's no good trying to put it off,' she said. 'I'm just going to do it and in an hour's time you're going to thank me.'

'No, I shan't,' I said. My face was red again. 'I'm not ready. I'm absolutely not ready.'

'Oh, balderdash.'

She let the letter flap shut. I heard the sound of her feet inside. The house went quiet.

I walked away, along the front, down the side, then turned again on to the patio at the back. I tried the French doors. They were still bolted.

I crossed the lawn and settled in the deck chair under the apple tree.

My heart was calm, not pumping, and my palms were cool, not sweating. I wasn't anxious. I was above me in the tree, sitting on one of the boughs, and I was looking down at me. I saw my hair hanging over the back of the deck chair, the ribs in my T-shirt, the buttons on my dress, my trainers with the laces not knotted but tucked inside the shoe.

Then I floated down from the tree and went back inside myself and I was looking up. Then I saw Emma's face above mine, looking down at me, and the apple tree behind her, with its green leaves and hard, round green bitter fruits, and the sky beyond, blue and dark with clouds like great piles of cotton wool scudding across.

'You can't put this off any longer,' said Emma with a smirk. 'He wants to speak to you, now, on the telephone. He's waiting. Come on.'

How am I going to get out of this? I thought. She's rung him, I'll have to go and speak to him, and in the future she'll say that whatever happened was her doing.

For a second or two, I seriously thought about saying no and just staying there in the deck chair and refusing to budge. Was she going to drag me inside by my hair and force me to speak to John by sticking pins in my legs? She couldn't make me. If I didn't want to go, she would just have to go in and explain this to John.

Then I realised something huge. Emma didn't have the power in this situation. I had the power. If I went in and picked up the phone, I was saving her from the embarrassment of explaining to John that I wasn't coming.

I decided I would do the noble thing and help her.

I got up, slowly. I had no intention of saying

anything yet. I'd let her keep on guessing until I actually picked up the phone.

I started to move slowly across the grass towards the door.

The phone was on the table in the hall. It lay on its side. It looked like a black bone.

'Go on,' said Emma.

All I could think of was me and him and that was a terrifying thought.

'It won't bite, you know,' she said. 'Promise.'

I picked up the phone. Nothing else I could do.

'Hello.'

'Hello' said John.

'Hello,' I said again.

'You've said hello already,' shouted Emma.

'Yes.'

'What was that?' said John.

'I was just saying yes,' I explained, 'as in, Yes, this is me, Phoebe.'

I put my free hand over the mouthpiece and pushed Emma away with my shoulder.

'Go away.'

'What?' said John, who had heard something despite the hand I had clamped over the phone.

'No, no, John, I didn't mean you. I was talking to somebody else.'

Emma started to shake. It was the shake of deep,

volcanic laughter, and in order to stop it coming out, she clamped a hand over her nose and mouth and squeezed her waist with her other arm.

'Excuse me, John.'

I put my hand over the mouthpiece once again. Emma was going to spoil everything. John was going to hear her laughing, and he was going to think we were just two silly girls who had egged each other on to make the call, and then he would hang up. Didn't she understand that this meant something to me?

'Shut up,' I shouted. Emma turned round and stared at me. She stuck out her jaw and widened her eyes. She called this her Oh, Madame! face.

'Are you there?' asked John.

'I'm just telling Emma not to make so much noise and to get out of my face.'

'She's making a lot of noise.'

Suddenly, Emma was shrieking again. I glared at her to be quiet.

'Are you coming over then?' I heard John saying.

'I'm sorry,' I said. 'What did you say?'

'Are you coming over?' he repeated. 'You know. Are you coming over to the house?'

'Coming over to your house?' I said.

Emma stared at me and nodded her head vigorously up and down.

'Yes,' I said.

'Yes,' said Emma, jumping up and punching the air.

'Yes,' said John at the other end of the line. 'Are you coming now?'

'All right,' I said.

'I'll see you in a while. Goodbye.'

I put the phone down and now I felt so incredibly happy, I threw my arms around Emma and she threw her arms around me and we shouted, 'Yes, yes, yes . . .' and we jumped up and down.

About an hour later, we walked up the Leary's concrete lane, me and Emma. The lane was yellow, pale yellow, and there were tiny ridges running across it from side to side. There was a barbed wire fence on the right and the field on the other side was filled with Mr Leary's herd of Jersey cows. They were chewing away as cows usually do. In the middle of the field there was an old standing stone with writing or marks of some sort on it. My dad had told me people came from miles around to see this. It was also meant to have special powers. If you had a wart, you put your hand on the stone and you walked anti-clockwise three times and the wart was gone by the next morning.

I could see the Leary house at the end of the lane. It was a brick built bungalow with two huge bow windows, one on either side of the front door, and an extension at the back which ran down towards the yard where the outbuildings and the sheds were clustered.

Although it was right in the country, Mrs Leary had the house like it was in a town. There was a lawn at the front with a fence and a gate and a concrete path which ran down to the front door. There were flower beds and in one corner there was a rockery with gnomes and windmills.

Inside the house something moved behind the curtains in the sitting room. One of John's older sisters or brothers, perhaps, or his terrifying grandmother. A moment later the door opened. It was John.

'He's got his ghetto blaster,' I said.

'I wonder why?' said Emma.

John put the machine down on the ground and touched something and the tinny sound of music in the open air drifted up the lane towards us.

'De de de de, dee, de-de,' Emma hummed, and I recognised this tune only I couldn't say its name. It was so frustrating.

'*It must be love, do-doh,*' sang Suggs.

Of course, 'It must be love,' Madness, of course I knew it.

'*It must be love, love, love, doh-do,*' Suggs sang, and I heard there was another voice singing with him, and I knew it was John.

I heard, '*Love is the best,*' and Emma's elbow dug

into my arm and she started to laugh, her laugh and the song joining together. I felt my knees trembling and my heart was in my mouth, and I heard Emma's laughing and it wasn't anything like any laugh I'd heard from her before. It wasn't full, or rich, or jeering, or uproarious; it was thin, it was uncertain, it was the laugh of someone who was amazed. I was amazed as well and my amazement grew stronger with every step which we took towards the gate. I was hearing the music loud now. It was booming in my ears. It was filling my head. I felt warm and happy and frightened and excited all at the same time.

'*Doh – doh,*' sang Suggs and John, while the trumpets blew.

John ran forward before my hand got to the latch on the other side of the gate. He pulled the gate back, and then, still singing along, he bent forward from the waist and bowed and motioned to me with his right arm to step in.

We stepped in. Still singing with the music, John ran past us, opened the front door, and bowing again, he motioned us to step in.

'I could get used to this,' said Emma and she went up the two steps and into the hall ahead of me.

'*It must be love, doh – doh,*

Love is the best . . .' John sang to me and smiled right into my face as I stepped up and went into the

Leary's front hall which smelt of strong perfume and apples and chocolate.

Happiness, happiness, happiness . . .

7 John

I saw John most days in the weeks that followed. Emma came out with us sometimes, but not always. She didn't like to be the goosegog, she said, but she was nice enough towards me and she didn't take exception to my new friendship. I think she quite liked John. She said he was a good influence on me. Once, she and John went off alone together for a cycle ride and they came back with a bunch of flowers which they had picked for me on the bog. As I had predicted, Emma believed that but for her intervention nothing would have happened between John and me, and I was quite happy to let her think that. What did I care? So long as she remained my friend. Big school was coming at the end of the summer, and I wanted to know I could rely on her then, and besides, I don't really like falling out with anyone.

I got on brilliantly with John. We didn't do much – just walked around and mucked about. We did kiss a couple of times. The best days were those when John mowed our lawn for Dad and got paid a pound an hour. When he finished we'd always walk across the fields with Tom and Fred to the nearest little shop and spend every last penny that he earned on sweets. Then we would go and lie under a big oak tree in a field full of sheep and scoff the lot. One day, which was very hot, we all got so stuffed we all fell asleep, and when we woke up, there were sheep ringed around us, staring at us with their yellow eyes and I could smell their warm grassy breath. Then Tom waved an arm; it terrified the sheep and sent them scattering in every direction. We spent the rest of the afternoon chasing after them, trying to herd them into a corner. We didn't have much success.

Later, the farmer who owned the field passed by with his dogs. He came and showed us how his dogs could round up the sheep in seconds. He asked us not to chase his animals. He gave each of us a fifty pence coin. We went back to the shop and bought another pile of sweets. Come evening, none of us wanted to eat our dinner and Mum was very cross when we told her why.

'You're each going to turn into a sweet,' she said grimly. 'And you'll have no teeth left by the time you're twenty-one.' That was the same evening that Mum told me, after supper this was, that my old best friend's mum had been on the phone earlier. Sylvia was coming to Ireland at the end of the summer, to stay with me for a whole fortnight. But because of John and that, I didn't really take this in.

What else did we do, John and I? Well, we walked up and down the High Street in town. We went to the cinema. We went bowling. We went swimming. We took Tom and Fred out for walks. We helped the boys with their base, repairing the roof, closing up the gaps in the walls, adding a wooden bolt to the door so it could be closed from the inside. Those lovely weeks of June and early July, we did this, we did that, but we did nothing really important. Like I said, we didn't go to Belfast or anything like that. Yet these times we spent together were always pleasant and nice and easy and friendly. We'd about three weeks of good times, I'd say.

The only thing that wasn't so brilliant was Mrs Leary. She didn't like me. She said I tramped dirt into her house and muddied her clean floors. She said I left the butter knife in the jam dish. Once, she even said I hadn't flushed the lavatory, which was a complete lie. She was very house-proud; so I gave her a tea towel with a poem written on it in praise of a house-proud housewife and relations looked up a bit after that.

8 The Twelfth

On the Twelfth of July, a lot of people go marching in Northern Ireland – like the men we met on the ferry coming over from Scotland. But a lot of other people don't like the marching, they leave, and John's family were part of this group. On the Twelfth of July, Mr and Mrs Leary always went to the south for the day, and this Twelfth, they had decided to spend at Rossnowlagh, a beach in Donegal. John asked me if I wanted to go with them, and Mum said I could. There would be just him and his parents; all John's siblings were doing something else. Of course Fred and Tom wanted to come as well but Mum stopped that.

'It's Phoebe's treat,' she said. 'Let your sister have some time without you two hanging around her and cramping her style.'

Perhaps it might have been better if they had come. I'd have had two allies at least and I wouldn't have felt so alone.

The car came at nine. Mr Leary, Michael, was driving, and Mrs Leary, Caroline as she now made me call her, sat beside him. I got into the back beside John.

'Hello, Phoebe, how are you?' said Caroline.

'Oh, I'm very well, thank you very much.' I was always very polite with Caroline.

I waved to Mum who had come out to say goodbye. We drove down our lane and turned on to the road heading in the direction of Donegal. There were a few questions from the front about my family. I said everyone was fine. Michael turned on the radio.

At Rossnowlagh, we drove down the slipway and on to the beach. There were already masses of cars on the sand because of the Bank Holiday and because it was a fine day.

'Is the tide going out?' Caroline asked, and Michael squinted at the shore, where children were splashing in the water. He said, 'I think so, yes.'

'We don't want to get caught by the tide coming in,' said Caroline.

I smiled as I imagined her in the car with the sea lapping around the door. She noticed this and must have guessed it was a wicked thought I had had, because next thing I saw her brows furrowing. I rather enjoyed that she knew I'd thought something of which she wouldn't approve, and, at the same time, that she also knew that she'd never get it out of me, what it was I'd thought.

Michael drove along the hard wet sand. There was

blue sky and grey water to the left, and car after car after car to the right. At last we found a place between two parked cars and reversed in. Michael turned off the engine. I wound down my window. I heard a news voice on the radio, and music, house music, I think. I also heard the tinkle of an ice-cream van and the distant cries of children.

I opened the door and got out and smelled the sea. I loved the smell of salt mixed with seaweed, the sharp clean air, the feel of the sand, cold and firm beneath my feet.

Michael opened the boot. He got out the wind break and began to hammer the staves into the sand.

'Why don't you help me?' Caroline called from the boot. She was lifting out a folding chair. 'In our family,' she added, 'we like everyone to pull their weight.'

My ears went red. I hadn't been there two minutes and already she was having a go. Despite the tea towel, she still didn't like me that much.

I smiled pleasantly at Caroline and I ran across to the boot. I knew better than to rise to the bait. John was behind his mother. He was looking down at the ground. He was as red in the face as me. Michael was hammering away at the staves of the wind break. He clearly wanted nothing to do with this.

'Let's get the table,' said John, and we lifted it out and unfolded its creaking aluminum legs.

'Coming in the sea?' said John.

'All right.'

He nipped into the car and I saw him struggling through the rear window as he changed. I know what the beach is like and what a pain it is changing so I had my costume already on. I just unbuttoned my dress and I was ready. I put my dress over the windbreak and sat down on the chair beside Caroline to take off my trainers.

'Had our cossie on already, had we?' said Caroline, looking up from her giant crossword puzzle. Michael began to whistle a tune. He was kneeling at the stove, trying to light it. 'You're just like me. You don't want anybody to see your big bottom.'

Caroline stared at me with her pale, round face. Her eyebrows were lovely arching shapes; she plucked them to get them like this. Her hands were big and she had heavy rings on all the fingers. Her nails were painted a light shade of pink. My mum wore varnish on her toes and sometimes her fingers, but she always wore red, bright red, the colour of a pillar box. If you're going to wear it, flaunt it, that was my mum's motto, and she didn't care for these pale insipid colours that gave the impression, as she put it, that the wearer didn't want to be noticed. Of course Caroline had such a way about her, it was impossible not to notice her; so she was the exception that proved Mum's rule.

'Let's have a look at your bottom,' Caroline said, craning sideways and staring at me. 'No, it really isn't *too* big.'

Was she trying to be nice, or was she saying my bottom was big like hers? I didn't know. That was Caroline. One never knew whether she was on the attack or not.

The car door slammed and I heard John saying, 'Come on.' I was relieved.

'Have a good time,' said Caroline. 'Don't drown.'

'Course not, Mum,' shouted John, good-humouredly.

We hurried down to the sea. The ocean was white and frothy on the edge, and green turning to grey further out.

'Last one in's a sissy,' shouted John. He went forward, lifting his feet high and splashing the water. He was wearing black trunks with arrows on the side. His body was very white and muscular. He was especially muscular across his back.

I went into the water after him, squealed and dashed back on to the sand. I don't like cold water.

'Come on,' shouted John. He had gone out a long way but because the beach at Rossnowlagh shelves so gently, the sea wasn't more than half way to his knees.

'It's freezing,' I called back.

'No, it isn't. It's lovely once you're in.'

'You won't splash?' I hated being splashed, hated it.

'Oh, come on,' he said, and he turned away and he started to walk out. 'It's lovely and warm.'

If he was so intent on getting out into the deep water, then he wasn't going to play silly games, was he? So I ran after him, and my goodness it was cold. By the time the sea was up to my ankles I wanted to turn round and run out. But I decided that as John was pressing on, I was going to press on after him. I kept running, gasping and shrieking and flapping my arms, the water splashing around me. The level of the water travelled up my shins, over my knees and up my thighs, and then I finally caught up with John.

'Ha!' he shouted and he turned with a huge grin on his face, and with his two hands he scooped a great lump of water and hurled it into my face.

'Surprise,' he shouted, and as the water hit my skin I saw I'd been duped by this act of walking out.

I shouted as the water hit me. Then I felt John take a shoulder and lift my leg up at the knee.

Although I didn't like splashing I could just about put up with it. But when I felt the grip of his hands, my mood changed. How dare he push me in! I felt angry, and me there on my own, no one on my side, and his mother being her usual rotten self to me.

I tumbled backwards and fell. First my body went

under, then my shoulders, and finally my head. The water closed over my face. I felt the sandy floor of the sea bed under me.

I put my feet down. I felt myself standing and then I heard myself shouting so angrily.

'That was horrible. That was a horrible thing to do. You horrible boy.'

At the same time, the bit of me that's above events and looks down on things was vaguely aware of some children who were behind John. They had turned to stare at me. They were expecting a fight.

And as soon as I saw these faces, I knew I should stop this.

But I didn't stop shouting. 'That was horrible,' I screamed, 'and I hate you!'

Then I noticed that I had my hand around John's leather necklace, and that I was tugging at it with all my strength.

From the part of me looking down on the scene came a warning; the leather would never snap and the fastener was a sturdy thing. I was just going to have to unscrew it at the back. It would take ages. John would be gone by the time I had the necklace off. And then where would I be? He wouldn't be there for me to give it back to him with everyone looking on. I would have to chase after him and I would look stupid.

But then, suddenly, to my amazement, the necklace

was in my hand. I knew I should stop this. I was not going to win. I was going to look stupid.

At the same time, I saw John was stepping backwards, getting ready to turn and run off. I didn't have long. I had to take my chance or that was it. So I ran forward and took his hand, and slapped the necklace into his palm.

'You can have your necklace back,' I screamed. I saw faces in the background, staring, adults as well as the children. And suddenly I saw how they saw me. I was a spoilt nasty brat.

John looked at me for a moment and then at his hand. I was waiting for him to say sorry. I was also hoping he was going to say sorry because then I could say sorry and then we could talk, and as we talked, we could walk away.

John opened his mouth and I was certain he was going to speak. But instead of a word, instead of the word sorry, his arm flew back and as it came forward he made a wordless noise, the noise which boys always make when they throw something.

A fraction of a second after this the necklace flew out of his hand. It travelled through the air and then fell with a plop into the sea.

I felt sick in my stomach.

John turned and began to walk away. I heard the children start to splash their parents and tumble in the sea. Everything was back to normal, for the onlookers that is.

I stood in the water for quite a long time. When I was absolutely certain no one was looking at me any more, I slowly walked towards where I believed the necklace had landed. I thought that if I went back and John saw it was hanging around my neck again, he wouldn't be angry any more. And if he wasn't angry any more, I wouldn't be angry any more, and it would be as if we hadn't had our argument.

I got to the spot. The water was well over my waist. I couldn't see the bottom because of the great clouds of sand stirred up by the sea. So I decided to find the necklace with my feet. I began to tread carefully. I felt a stone. I had to find it. It was a matter of life and death. I went on searching, carefully placing one foot in front of the other. I found a shell and another stone, but I never found the thin length of leather with the polished dolphin hanging off it.

Then I heard a voice calling, 'Phoebe, lunch.'

I turned and saw John on the beach. He wore a pair of shorts and a T-shirt. His feet were bare.

'Lunch,' he called again.

His voice wasn't angry; it was cold, uninterested. I turned in the water and started to walk towards him. He walked away up the beach leaving me following along behind, back towards the car where his mother and father were waiting.

I got my towel from the wind break, wrapped it round myself and then went to the table.

'We've started,' said Caroline, 'I hope you don't mind.'

She sounded quite gleeful. I sat down on the stool at the place that was laid for me.

'No avocado here,' she said, handing me the potato salad.

'No, thank you,' I said, 'I don't eat potato salad.' This was true; I hate potato salad.

I ate a hard boiled egg, a piece of bread and butter, and a spoon of yogurt with cucumber chopped up in it. Then I put my knife and fork together. I didn't want to eat any more.

'Not hungry?' asked Caroline.

'No,' I said.

'I thought the sea gave you cubs an appetite, but he's not eating either.'

She pointed at John's plate and I saw he had hardly touched the potato salad or the slices of ham which he had taken.

Later, when John was helping his mother with the drying and I was wiping the table, I heard Caroline whispering to her son but loudly enough so that I could hear, 'Why aren't you talking? Have you had a row?'

After lunch, I spread my towel on the sand and lay down and dozed in the sun. John sat in the car and listened to a Grand Prix motor race on the radio. Michael and his wife played cards.

By four o'clock the beach was jammed.

'I think we should make a move now, don't you?' suggested Michael, 'before the roads fill up when everyone goes home.'

We packed the car and drove up the ramp. With the sun shining down hard all day, the tarmac on the road had gone sticky and there was a strong smell of tar. A long queue of cars waited to make the turn to Bally-shannon road. While we waited, Caroline kept fanning herself with her crossword book and saying, over and over again, 'I'm glad we're getting out now. It's going to be murder later on.'

We got to my house at six.

'Thank you,' I said.

'You're welcome,' said Caroline.

'Bye,' said John, 'see you.' He said it quickly, without any feeling.

As I was getting out, Mum came over.

'Do you want to come in for tea?'

'I don't think so,' said Caroline. 'Michael's got to get back to his animals, don't you, Michael?'

The car drove off down the lane and Mum said, 'Nice day?'

'Oh, yeah.'

I definitely didn't want to talk about it.

'I've got to hang up my towel and my swimsuit,' I said, and I waved the rolled-up towel in the direction of the washing line.

'Is something the matter? Something is the matter, isn't it?'

At the sound of her words my eyes filled with tears. Then the tears were rolling down my cheeks and my mum was folding me in her arms. I let out a great sob as I threw my towel on the ground and I pushed my face against her side.

'You better tell me what happened?' she said, and I told her. Everything.

In the evening, Emma and Linda came over. It was Mum's idea. She did it to cheer me up.

Emma noticed straight away that the necklace was gone but she didn't say anything until we were alone in my bedroom.

'Where's the necklace, then?' she said. She was lying on the bed across from mine. It was just like her to be that blunt.

'John pushed me into the sea, and I hate cold water and I don't know if he knows that but he should. Anyway, I got very cross with him. I took off his necklace and I made this big thing of giving it back to

167

him and everyone around us was watching. But instead of just going off with his necklace when I gave it to him, which is what I thought he'd do – do you know what he did? He threw it way out to sea, like it didn't matter to him, and nothing mattered to him, and I certainly didn't matter to him. Then we had this horrible lunch when nobody said anything, and I could feel Caroline looking at me all the time and I knew she was thinking, Phoebe and John had a quarrel! Good! I never did like her. Then we drove back and John said goodbye like nothing had happened, and now I'm here and I never, ever want to see him again and I don't imagine I ever will.'

'Oh well,' said Emma, when I finished. She was lying back on the pillow and staring up at the ceiling. 'I wouldn't cry over him. The world is full of Johns and there's bound to be another one along soon enough, just like a bus.'

I guessed Emma had heard someone else saying this (probably Linda). But I was certain Emma believed it. A friendship doesn't work? Oh, well, get another! That was her way but it wasn't mine.

'Well, now it's just us again, as it should be,' Emma announced.

She fell asleep soon after, but I couldn't sleep. I couldn't stop thinking about this last remark. I knew that as my friend she should have wanted me to be happy with John. But clearly she didn't want this. Then I realised she'd just been tolerating my friendship with John. She hadn't really approved although she said she did. Even when she went off to the bog to pick flowers with John, she was just pretending that she liked him. She was waiting for it to end and now it had.

Happiness is a funny thing. It comes into your life when you don't know it's coming, and it then goes out of your life in the same way. There doesn't seem to be any sense to it.

PART THREE
Frozen Out

1 Unwelcome visitors

After a couple of days, the thought of John didn't really hurt me any more. If I thought about him all I got was a little ache, and after a few more days, even that healed over. Within a week or so, I'd recovered completely, and my life was back to what it had been. I saw Emma almost every single day and we often stayed over in each other's house.

Several weeks after Rossnowlagh, it was nearly the middle of August now, I woke up in Emma's house one morning, in the bed on the other side of the room from Emma's bed, and the very first thing I heard was the song of a thrush.

Arthur had introduced us to the thrush. Arthur now practically lived in Linda's house. Since I'd started hanging around with Emma again, we'd done a bit of bird watching with him. It was his hobby. I think Arthur saw the bird watching as a way of making friends with me and Emma.

'That's a song thrush,' I called out to Emma, but she didn't hear me.

I squinted at the curtains. I wanted to see what sort of a day it might be outside. Not much light, as far as I was able to see, so it was probably just another grey Fermanagh day. It had been pretty grey since that awful day at the beach. Normally, I wouldn't really have minded. I mean, I was used to this. But this morning the weather worried me. In a few days Sylvia was coming from London. I hadn't seen her for a whole year now. But I'd written. I'd told her we'd have a great time when she came; we'd swim and sail and ride and walk. But of course, if it was grey and wet, like today, we'd be cooped up indoors all the time. With my brothers screaming and shouting. Which was hardly a reason to come to Crookedstone.

Mum says it's ridiculous to feel responsible for the weather when one has guests. Does anyone in London apologise to visitors if it's raining or snowing? Of course not. But in Ireland, for some reason, you do feel responsible for the weather.

I started to feel distinctly uncomfortable. I wanted to put these thoughts out of my mind, and Sylvia along with them. But before I could stop myself, my heart started to race, and I knew I couldn't avoid it.

The thing was, I was looking forward to Sylvia coming; in fact I could hardly wait. But I was also dreading it.

Sylvia was my best friend in London but now I was

older and so was she. I was also terrified that we wouldn't have anything to talk about, that we wouldn't have anything in common any more, that we'd just sit, hour after hour, day after day, with not a word to say to each other, with each of us praying and begging for the holiday to end.

I was also worried about something else. This was even more dreadful than the idea of having nothing to say.

Sylvia was my best friend in London. But now Emma was my best friend here. When Sylvia arrived, I'd have two best friends in the same place and at the same time. It wasn't going to work. They'd both want me, and of course it was going to have to be Emma that I ignored. Inevitably. Sylvia was coming from London. Mum would make me be with her all the time. This would be fine so long as Sylvia was staying with us, but after she left and school started, there'd be hell to pay with Emma. At least John was out of the picture. If he were around, I was certain I wouldn't have been able to cope at all. I'd have just run away and hidden under my bed.

'Girls, I'm going out for a while,' Linda shouted from below.

A second later I heard the sound of Linda on the stairs and then the door burst open and there was Linda standing in the doorway.

'Emma, are you awake?' she said.

Emma sighed, and said grumpily, 'No, I'm asleep.'

'I don't want you to lie in bed all morning,' said Linda. 'You're not going to lie in bed all morning, are you, Emma?'

This was a new thing with Linda. Or maybe I should say, this was a new thing with Emma. She had taken to lying in at weekends and Linda had taken against it. Linda said it depressed her if anyone was in bed after ten o'clock, even on a Sunday morning. Linda said life was for living, not for sleeping, and she insisted on her daughter getting up and doing things.

Emma argued she was growing and she needed her beauty sleep. She said Linda's obsession with early rising was the last gasp of her Protestant work ethic. And finally, she said Linda was just repeating her childhood, because when she was young she had served behind her father's shop counter every morning, even on school mornings.

Linda and Emma were far sharper with each other than I and my mother were. Nor were they shy about using special or private things which they knew about each other to score a point, or as a way to hurt one another. They also seemed to really enjoy fighting, and Emma seemed to want me around to see it. I hated it.

'Get up,' said Linda, stepping into the room.

'Wha'?' murmured Emma.

'I want you up, do you understand?' said Linda, the level of her voice rising. 'I'm going shopping and when I get back I expect to find you dressed. You as well, Phoebe.'

'Yes,' I said.

Without appearing to hear me, Linda sailed right on, 'You girls can help me unpack the car, put away the groceries and then we're going to make a packed lunch. We're going for a walk. It's not a bad day outside.'

'Oh no,' moaned Emma.

'Emma, I've told you. No dossing at weekends. Have you any homework these holidays for the new school?'

A pause and then, after she had kept the pause going for as long as was humanly possible, Emma finally said, 'Yes.'

'When are you going to do it?'

'Don't know.'

'You can make a start on it now!'

'Do I have to?'

'Absolutely. And Phoebe, I expect you have some as well.'

'Yes,' I said, 'yes, I do.'

'Right up you get then, Em. Come on, feet on the floor, feet on the floor.'

I threw back my duvet and got straight out of bed.

'Come on, madam, I've had just about enough of this.'

Linda whipped the duvet off the bed, revealing Emma curled on the mattress.

'Oh no,' she moaned, 'it's cold.'

Emma pulled her night dress over her feet and shrunk into a tight ball.

'Oh, get up,' said Linda, a certain humour in her voice. She pulled the curtains back. Outside it was indeed a grey day.

'Linda, give me back my duvet,' Emma pleaded.

She was awake now.

'Get up.'

Emma was defeated. Her long, pale legs snaked across the mattress, curled over the edge and went to the floor.

'You can stand up. Come on, I want to see you stand up.'

'Oh, I hate you,' Emma shouted, and with surprising energy, she swung her body upright and stood up.

'See,' Linda said triumphantly, 'that wasn't so bad, was it?'

She took her daughter's arm and began to move her towards the door.

'Right, go and splash your face. Go on. Hurry.'

'All right,' grumbled Emma, and she disappeared through the door.

'Phoebe, get up, get dressed, have breakfast.'

'Absolutely,' I said.

'You're worse than Adolf Hitler . . .' Emma shouted from the bathroom, 'and Joseph Stalin, and Benito Mussolini . . .'

'Yeah, yeah,' said Linda, and she hurried from the room.

Ten minutes later we were downstairs at the breakfast table. Emma thrust her hand and then her arm deep into the packet of Rice Krispies and began to root about inside.

'Yes, yes, yes,' she shouted and she pulled out a small, red plastic figure.

'I hope you've washed your hands,' I said.

'I just read a report in the paper,' she said, 'that environmental health officers tested a bowl of peanuts on a pub bar and found twelve different samples of wee. You see everyone, after having a wee, saw the bowl and thought, Oh, I'll have a peanut.'

I was screwing up my face in disgust when I saw someone at the back door.

It was a man in a donkey jacket. There were two other men behind him.

As I turned the man in the donkey jacket lifted an arm and smiled at me through the glass.

'Who's that?' said Emma.

'I don't know.'

'Did Linda say anything about anyone coming to do anything in the garden or anything?'

'When you were asleep? No.'

'Well then, you'd better open the door,' she said.

I went and opened the door.

'Good morning,' the man began, 'we're from Green Fingers.'

I looked at him.

'We're a gardening service. We're new in the area. We couldn't help noticing as we drove past, the large and very lovely garden you have here and we wanted to introduce ourselves because we wonder if there's anything we can do for you.'

'You'll have to speak to my mother,' called Emma.

She was putting the little Rice Krispies figure on top of the dresser with the other figures she had collected.

'Is your mother by any chance at home?' asked the man in the donkey jacket.

'No.'

'I wonder if I could leave our card?' he continued.

He pulled a card from a bundle and handed it to me.

'We do fencing, we lay patios, we cut grass, we make and weed beds, we build ponds, we fell trees; we do maintenance and landscaping and no job is too big or too small.'

I took the card and looked at it. It said:

Green Fingers, the complete gardening service.

That was all there was on the card.

'Excuse me.' This was not Donkey jacket, but the man behind him who wore a boiler suit. 'Could I use your toilet?'

I didn't know what to say but I heard Emma saying, 'I suppose.'

'Where is it?' he asked, wiping his boots carefully on the door mat.

Emma pointed into the hall. 'Round the corner, first door on the left,' she said.

Boiler suit disappeared into the hall.

'Very lovely place you have here,' said Donkey jacket. 'Beautiful grounds and lovely house. How old is it, if you don't mind my asking?'

'About a hundred years,' said Emma.

'And what was it?'

'What do you mean?' said Emma.

'Was it a special house, a station master's house, a school master's house, or something like that? It looks like the sort of place that might get written about.'

'I think it was an estate house. The landlord built it.'

'It isn't listed, is it? It looks as if it might be.'

'I don't know.'

'I only ask because you don't see many of these lovely old houses in Fermanagh. Everyone seems to live in bungalows nowadays.'

I heard the cistern flushing and Boiler suit returned.

'Lovely banister rods,' he said. 'They've been hand-turned, did you know that? Lovely stained glass window on the return, as well. I'm sorry to trouble you, but I couldn't have a glass of water, could I? Then I promise we'll clear off and let you get on with your breakfast in peace.'

Emma filled a glass at the sink and handed it to Boiler suit. He lent against the work top, drank the water, handed the glass back.

'Well, thank you,' he continued, 'and you won't forget to mention us to your mother. I didn't get the name.'

'Turtle,' said Emma.

'Turtle. I bet you have to put up with a few rare comments about that name at school.'

'Not really,' said Emma coolly. 'I mean, she's called Phoebe.' Emma pointed at me. 'That's far worse.'

'Well, thank you for your hospitality.'

Boiler suit and Donkey jacket stamped towards the door. 'I hope we'll see you again.'

They went out, joined the third man who'd been left waiting outside, and drove off.

'Goodness me,' said Emma. 'Staff! You just can't get them nowadays.'

2 Big trouble

Linda pulled up in the car outside. The horn honked twice.

'Portering duties,' moaned Emma from the sink. 'Her demands are incessant, aren't they?'

We went outside. The day was cold and grey. The car boot was open. It was filled with groceries.

'Hello,' said Linda.

We carried the lot inside and put everything on the table. Then we started to put everything away.

'What's this?' I heard Linda asking.

'I don't know. What's what?' said Emma.

'It's grease,' said Linda. 'How did that get in here?'

It was just the tiniest line of black along the edge of the work top.

'It must have been that man,' I said.

'What man?'

'There was a man. He wanted some water.'

'A man, who?'

'Well, there were three of them.'

'Three!' shrieked Linda. 'Phoebe, you'd better tell me about it.'

I told her about the men from Green Fingers; then I took down the card from the pin board where I had put it and gave it to her.

'What's this?'

'It's their card.'

'It doesn't have a telephone number. It just has the name, no address, no telephone number.'

'Oh, yes,' I said.

'Haven't I been through this with you before, Emma?'

Emma was kneeling in front of the freezer drawer, her back towards us. She had taken everything out of the drawer and was now re-packing it. As this was an unnecessary task it was obvious she didn't want to join in the conversation. I could see her point. I wasn't enjoying it either. There was an edge to Linda's voice. She was talking politely, but any moment now she was going to explode and start shouting or throwing things.

'Emma, did you hear me? I'm talking to you,' said Linda coldly.

'Yes.'

'Turn round.'

Emma swivelled round on her knees. She stared at the floor.

'Haven't I explained that to you? Because of Arthur we have to be doubly careful when anybody comes to the house that we don't know.'

185

So Arthur was involved in this. I recalled now how he had said this was not a good area where Linda lived. Too many Irish flags on the lamp posts, he said. He wasn't really meant to come, it was too close to the border, and if his officers found out he'd be in trouble. In fact, now I came to think about it, he'd said this half a dozen times or more.

And then, having said all this, he always added that he didn't give a tinker's curse about his officers, and that he'd keep coming out anyway.

Then I realised these men were something to do with Arthur – or that's what Linda thought.

'Emma, will you look at me when I'm talking,' I heard Linda saying in the coldest, frostiest voice I'd ever heard her using, and I knew this was going to be much worse than the worst 'Stranger Danger' lecture.

My knees trembled and I watched Emma raise her eyes slowly.

'You listen to this as well, Phoebe. If you are in the house on your own and three men who you do not know come to the door, you do not open the door, do you? No. You say, "My mother's busy" and you tell them to come back later.'

'Phoebe opened the door before I had time to think. She just ran up and opened it.'

I could hardly believe my ears. Emma was saying this was my fault. But it was she who told me to open the door. 'Well then, you'd better open the door.' Those were her exact words.

'Did you, Phoebe?'

'I did,' I said, my face going red as I spoke, 'but Emma told me to open the door.'

'Oh really. And if Em told you to jump out the window you'd do that as well?'

'No.' That wasn't what I was saying at all. But before I could organise my thoughts and get my words out, Emma was speaking.

'I told you not to open the door, but you did it before you heard me.' Emma said this very firmly.

'No, I did not, that's untrue.'

'Well, whatever happened,' interrupted Linda, 'you should both know you should not let men you don't know into the house, period. Is that clear? Is that CLEAR?'

'Yes, Mum.'

It was the first time I'd ever heard Emma call Linda Mum.

'Phoebe, do you understand?'

'Yes.'

We put away the rest of the groceries in silence. When we finished I ran upstairs, fetched my toothbrush and my school bag and came down again to the kitchen.

I found Linda at the kitchen table, moving the palms of her hands on the wooden surface in large circles.

Emma was in the front room practising the scales on her recorder which surprised me because she had said to me that she hated the instrument and she was giving it up.

'I've got to go home now,' I said.

'Aren't you coming out with us?'

'I've got a lot of homework for the new school,' I said.

'It's the holidays.'

Linda said this very quietly and she stared at her hands as she circled them on the table. She sounded like she was about to cry.

'I've got to do a project on the Nile and I think I should make a start,' I said, which was true.

'That's very conscientious of you, Phoebe.'

'I've got Sylvia coming, you see, next week, and I think it would be good to get it out of the way.'

'Oh yes, you've got your friend from London, I'd forgotten. Do you think there'll be enough for her to do here?'

She stared at her hands as if they were the most interesting things in the world.

'I think so.'

Emma's recorder piped next door.

'So, I'd better be off then,' I said.

'Do you want a lift?' Linda looked up and I saw that her eyes had great big wet tears in them. Whatever this was about, it was to do with Arthur.

'No, thank you. I'll walk it. The exercise will do me good.'

'You sure you don't want to stay with us?'

'No, I really think I ought to go.'

'Aren't you going to say goodbye to Emma?'

'Not when she's doing her scales. She only does five minutes practise a year. I wouldn't want to interrupt that.'

I went out and shut the door. I was glad to get out of there.

I climbed the gate and jumped down on to the old lane. I began to walk towards home. For a moment or two I didn't think about anything. Then, a rush of thoughts:

. . . That phone conversation I had with Mum, when I rang her from the swimming pool on the day John first came to lunch, when she said it was important to widen one's circle; Mum never referred to the conversation again, but she was absolutely right, of course. I didn't really listen then. It's so hard to listen to parents. They're so dull in comparison to one's friends.

And what really happened with John? He threw me in the sea. I was angry. He shouldn't have thrown me in. But was I right to be that angry? Probably not. And not for as long as I was, either. And then I threw his necklace back at him. Well, that finished it. I came home. Saw Emma. 'Well,' she said, 'now it's just us again, as it should be.' Course she would say that. That's what she wanted, wasn't it? She was waiting for the split to happen, wasn't she? Course she was, though she kept that hidden. What else did she mean? 'Now it's just us again, as it should be.' But why did I go along with it? Couldn't I have gone back to John and made up? Course not. Not after having given his dolphin back. Or could I? Could I not have gone back? Said sorry. It would have been awful. Dead embarrassing. The very idea of going to his house, Caroline smirking, an awkward conversation on the door step – it made my skin creep. Could I really have gone through that? No, I didn't think I could.

But I was straying from the point. I had to go back. Go back to the talk Emma and I had in the bedroom. I was a coward, wasn't I, to go with that and say nothing? I took the easy way out. Emma was delighted, naturally, to have me again, hers, hers to lead. Phoebe, Nicola and Sarah were the foot soldiers; Emma was the General. She was General Turtle. I was Private Rodgers. I was a fool. Fool, fool, fool. How could I? 'Now it's just us again, as it should be.' As it should be! What did 'As it should be' mean? It was nonsense. What she actually meant was that everything was as *she wanted it*. That's what she meant. That's what she got.

And I've given my friendship. Unstintingly. Without

question. And then what does she do? She tells a lie. She says I did something I didn't do. She says I let these Green Fingers people in, when I didn't. She was the one who told me to let them in. That's what actually happened. It was her house. She was in charge. But she said I did it. And Linda believed her. Now Linda thinks I brought in these ones who've got it in for Arthur. And the reason she thinks this is because Emma lied.

Emma saw Linda's fury coming. She knew it was going to be terrible. So she blamed me. That was my reward for being her friend. 'It's just us again, as it should be.' That was rubbish. We were friends only for as long as it suited her. And then when it no longer suited, she lied.

Oh, Sylvia, thank goodness, thank goodness, thank goodness you are coming, I thought. Thank goodness I have you to look forward to. Someone to walk with, someone to talk with. I would introduce her to Emma, I decided, and I'd enjoy that. 'This is my friend Sylvia. Have a good look at her, Emma, because you're only going to see her this once.' Yes, that's what I was going to say and I hoped it would sicken her. She could stick to Sarah and Nicola. No, better still, I'd have Sarah and Nicola over to meet Sylvia, and I'd deliberately not invite Emma. That would sicken her more – which she deserved. She wasn't my friend any more. She was a liar. And it was unfair, infuriatingly unfair, this whole thing. She was a monster. Yes, Emma was a monster and the sooner Sylvia got here and rescued me from her the better . . .

3 Plans go wrong

What is it they say about the best laid plans? Two days before she was due to fly to Belfast, Sylvia got appendicitis. Sylvia's mum said Sylvia was very upset. So she was going to keep the ticket, and after Christmas, if Sylvia felt like it, perhaps she would come out then.

I stood at Mum's side throughout the call.

'Oh dear,' said Mum, when she put the phone down, 'that is disappointing, but at least she's going to be all right.'

This was Mum, talking to get me talking, and hoping that if she got me talking, I'd forget my troubles. I had a long face on me and she knew I was upset.

'I'm glad she's all right,' I said, because I knew that's what Mum expected me to say.

'Listen,' I heard Mum suggest. 'I think it's time for a cup of cocoa and a Jaffa cake.'

'Yes,' I agreed, without much enthusiasm. When I was younger and I had a fight with one of my brothers, or I cut my knee, or I broke a toy, a little treat cheered me up. But cocoa and a Jaffa cake weren't going to make this better. This was beyond that. I had a friend and she had lied about me to her mother. And now Sylvia wasn't coming. This was worse than losing John, worse, worse, worse, because I had now lost my ready-made excuse: 'I'm sorry, Emma, I'd love to see you but Sylvia's here . . .'

Emma'd be up to see me in a day or two, and what was I supposed to do then? Act as if nothing had happened? Carry on as before?

'I don't want any cocoa,' I said.

'Don't you?'

She looked at me, her head down, so that her eyes and my eyes were level with one another. This was a recent development. She probably did it because I was taller. Or perhaps because she had read in some magazine that eye contact is important.

'Are you sure there isn't something else worrying you?'

I shook my head. I hadn't told her about Emma and the lie – and yet because she was my mum, I felt she *ought* to know, she *ought* to have guessed. She always used to be able to see right inside my head. On top of the betrayal by Emma, on top of the disappointment I felt about Sylvia, now there was this. My mum didn't love me any more. If she'd loved me, she'd have understood, she'd have guessed. But she hadn't, so she didn't love me.

'I don't want any cocoa,' I said.

Mum squinted at me, trying to work out what I was thinking.

'Don't stare at me,' I said.

'I'm not, I'm just looking at you. There's a difference between staring and looking.'

There was a long pause and then she said, 'What is the matter with you?'

'Nothing.'

'Nothing! Are you sure? You've got the longest face I've ever seen.'

'No.' I tried to sound cool, calm and collected. 'Nothing's the matter.'

Either she understood what I was feeling and she showed it, or she said nothing. That's all I wanted.

'What's happening with Emma? We haven't seen her, have we, for a while. Have you had an argument with her or something?'

'She's practising her recorder a lot,' I said. I stepped back towards the door. 'I'm going to my room.'

Mum hadn't understood and I wanted out.

Upstairs, I threw myself down on the bed and lay there. I felt a first twinge of pain inside. It was like a nick, like a paper cut, the sort of thing you have to look quite hard to find because it's so small. Yet it hurt, and as I lay there, it throbbed more and more.

*

The evening of the following day we got a visit. Linda and Emma nosed through the front door, though normally they always came in the back way.

I was in the kitchen playing Tetris on the Game Boy. I heard Linda's voice in the hall. I heard my mum. I heard Emma. I decided I wouldn't get up. I wouldn't go out. I decided I would just go on with my game, matching the falling shapes to the spaces at the bottom of the screen.

They came into the kitchen and Mum said, 'Aren't you going to say hello?'

'Hello,' I said. I didn't look up. 'I'm playing Tetris. Mum and me are having a competition. I'm on level ten. She's still on level eight.'

This was true – and now that I had made my point, I felt free to look up. I saw Emma was the same, with her long, sharp face framed by her long black hair, but the Linda I now saw in my kitchen was not the woman to whom I had said goodbye a few days earlier. That woman was still plump despite the diet. This woman was light and thin and brittle. Her skin was stretched tight over her bones, so tight, I imagined, that with a sharp jab of the finger the skin would break. Linda's eyes were bright and shining and a little bloodshot, and the skin had been rubbed red around her nose. Linda had been crying, crying and crying and crying, and to cover this up she had put on far more make-up than usual which only drew attention to the fact that she'd been crying. She looked terrible.

'I'll make the tea,' said Mum, and she plugged in the kettle.

'Hello,' I heard. It was a quiet, rather furtive greeting addressed by Emma to me. I looked up and nodded back at her. Emma pulled out a kitchen chair and sat down and squinted sideways at me. She had an odd look on her face. It said to me that there was something awful happening. She also rolled her eyes over towards her mother a couple of times.

Then I heard a sob. I looked over. Linda's eyes were big and wet. There were tears streaming down her cheeks. I looked back at my friend and she arched her eyebrows. Oh boy, this gesture seemed to be saying, mothers, they're just too much sometimes! She appeared to have forgotten what had happened the other day. As far as she was concerned, everything was back to the way it was before the lie.

Mum asked what was the matter and Linda began her story. I played Tetris but I listened. After I had said goodbye and gone home, Linda found herself thinking about the men I had let in. The card they left had no telephone number, no address, no details of any sort, as she had noticed. The more she looked at this, and the more she thought about these men, the more worried she became.

Eventually she decided to tell Arthur over the phone. Arthur came straight round to her house. He asked Emma to describe the men.

The police, he explained to Linda, and now Linda explained to us, had been in touch with his Commanding Officer. Apparently Arthur's name was on a list. The address on the list was not Arthur's home address – he lived with his mother just round the corner from where his wife and his two children lived. The address on the list was Linda's address.

At this very moment, Arthur was in the barracks. He had been told to report for an interview. He had been told that a policeman would be present during the interview. Arthur was in trouble, trouble in the Northern Ireland sense.

Someone was looking for him – the three fake gardeners who had come to the house, to be precise. Somehow, all at once, the army and the IRA and the police, everyone had got wind of Arthur and Linda, and it was not just his fate but their joint fate that was being decided at that moment in the barracks.

'But you don't know that for certain and nor does he,' said Mum. She put the brown teapot in the middle of the table on a mat. Four mugs and the milk jug followed. 'Who knows what's being said to Arthur? Maybe they're talking to him about something entirely different.'

Linda shook her head and blew her nose. 'No, no,' she shouted. 'From the moment Phoebe opened the door, that was the end of this, that was the end of this.'

Mum ignored that.

'I don't think anything's certain,' said Mum, 'until Arthur tells us what's happening.' She lifted the teapot and began to pour the tea.

'Why don't we play with the Sega Mega Drive,' said Emma.

'All right.'

We went into the front room, turned on the television and began to play Sonic 1. We took turns.

We noted the scores in silence.

Neither of us wanted to say anything. If we talked, then eventually we would have to talk about what had happened. I didn't want to do that, not because I was frightened of an argument, but because I was afraid of losing my temper completely. I was calm on the outside but inside I was shaking with anger.

Em, I guess, was just grateful for the silence because she knew she'd done wrong. I mean, how could she fail to recognise that?

There was a lot of talking in the kitchen and then the telephone rang a couple of times. I heard Linda talking on the phone. I heard Linda crying and shrieking. I heard my mum talking to Linda, her voice calm and soothing.

After a while things died down in the kitchen and I offered to get us juice and chocolate Digestives.

'Oh, wicked,' said Emma in her friendly voice. She obviously thought I was thawing.

I went down the hall and opened the kitchen door. I saw that Linda was where I'd left her, sitting at the table. But in the hour since I'd last seen her, she'd shrunk again. Unhappiness makes one smaller as surely as Alice's potion.

I saw Linda's face was wet from crying. She let out a terrible sob.

'It's all right,' I heard my mum saying. 'This is just temporary. Everything will work out, I promise.'

Arthur had telephoned earlier and spoken to Linda. He told her his name was on a list. The IRA were looking to kill him. The Army were worried. They told him he was not to go to Linda's any more. She lived too close to the border. He was too vulnerable in her house. They also told him that although he did not live with his wife, he was still married to his wife. The Army said they did not approve of his relationship with Linda as long as he remained married. He was not only forbidden to visit the house, he was also forbidden to see Linda again.

I walked towards the door carrying a tray with the glasses of juice and a plate of biscuits. Linda heard me as I passed. She opened her eyes and looked at me. It was a strange look. Next thing she let out a terrible sob. Mum was standing behind her and she put her arms around Linda and squeezed her tight.

I opened the kitchen door and went back to the hall. Now Mum knew about Arthur and that, now everything was out in the open, I felt better, yes, not much, just a bit. I was still furious with Emma. She had lied. Emma believed she was the world's greatest friend, and she had got me and Sarah and Nicola to believe this. But when push came to shove, what did she do? She was happy to sacrifice a friend in order to keep in with her mother.

However, in a way it was good to know this, because now I knew what she was *really* like, I wouldn't worship her any more. I was free. Now I could be her friend because I chose to be her friend. I could take her for what she was. I knew what to watch out for now. I knew never to trust her. And she knew I'd seen her for what she was as well. That's why she was here, while Linda cried in the kitchen. She wanted to make up. Well, we would make up, I decided. I didn't mind. I was happy to be friends. But not like we were before.

I barged through the door like a cowboy going into a saloon.

'Right!' I shouted. 'The chocolate Digestives are on me.'

Then I put the tray down, drew an imaginary pistol from an imaginary holster and fired it in to the air.

4 Piercing

The next day I asked Mum if I could have my ears pierced.

'All right,' said Mum, 'you can have your ears pierced.' She was sitting at the table in the garden doing a jigsaw puzzle with Fred.

'Oh, thank you, Mum, thank you.'

I'd been begging for months, and now she'd said yes, at last, I could hardly believe it.

'I don't think you've been very happy,' she said, as she fitted Cornwall into its place on the end of England. 'You deserve a treat. I hope it cheers you up. But promise me you'll turn the sleepers every day, you'll look after yourself.'

'Oh yes,' I promised, 'oh yes.'

The next morning, when Dad went in to work, I went with him. He took me to 'Pampers'. It was a beauty parlour with a sauna and a solarium and a Jacuzzi. Mum had done some research and found this was the best place in town to have it done.

My dad told a woman in a white coat I wanted my

ears pierced. The woman stood me in front of a big mirror and made little marks with a Biro on my lobes.

'Are you happy with those marks?' said the woman in the white coat.

'Oh yeah.'

'You're not even looking,' said Dad. 'Will you be happy with earrings where those marks are?' said Dad, folding up the paper he was reading and coming across. 'Or do you want them higher or lower?'

'No, I like them,' I said, and this time I looked.

'Do you want sleepers or studs?'

'Sleepers,' said Dad, who had been briefed by Mum.

'Sleepers,' I said.

The woman took me into a little room. There was music playing, a smell of perfume. I felt my stomach tightening and my heart going faster and faster. My palms were hot and I wiped them on my dress.

'Don't worry,' said the woman, 'it won't hurt, I promise.'

The woman turned away and started fiddling with something. I glimpsed what looked like a gun. The woman turned back and I knew the moment had come. I was terrified and delighted. I felt something clamp on my ear. The woman squeezed the trigger. There was a small sharp pain. The woman whipped the gun around to the other lobe. Another small sharp pain.

'We're done,' she said.

I ran to the mirror and lifted my hair. Two small circles of gold dangled from my lobes.

'Oh wow!' I said.

'Very lovely,' said Dad to me, a few minutes later, as I turned my head from side to side and showed him the sleepers.

'Are you happy?'

When I said, 'Yes,' he messed my hair like a kid and I shied away.

'Don't,' I said.

He turned to the counter and opened his cheque book.

'How much?' he said.

'Ten pounds.'

'What!' said Dad with mock horror. 'Any chance we could negotiate a reduction?' he said, which was very Dad of him.

'I don't think the boss'd be too happy about that,' said the woman, and smiled at me.

She was young, with a lot of brown foundation on her face and very bright blue eyes. I hadn't noticed her until now but then I had been rather wrapped up in myself.

Then I found myself wondering if that was the crack with Emma? She was so caught up with something, she didn't notice how she got me blamed for something I hadn't done. No, that was impossible. Her action was deliberate. She knew exactly what she was doing.

Funnily enough, suddenly, I could see why she'd done it. It was all very well being treated as an adult, as Emma was by Linda – being allowed to set your own bedtime, being encouraged to express your opinions, being taken to Belfast and allowed to choose whatever clothes you wanted – but when Linda went ballistic, she tore into Emma exactly as if she were an adult. I'd only seen it once or twice and it was horrible. She just went on and on until Em burst into tears. That's why Emma lied. It was to stop her mother being angry.

I went outside with Dad. We walked down to the newspaper offices together. He asked me in, I said no. I had to go to the chemist for Mum; then I was going to swim, and she was turning up later at the pool with the boys to collect me.

'All right then,' said Dad. He lent forward to kiss me and I said, 'Don't.'

He looked sad but it was too risky in case anyone saw.

'You're growing up too quickly. You're not the little girl I used to dandle on my knee.' He smiled at me. 'Got to get some of those pills they've just brought out to stop children growing.'

'In your dreams, Dad.'

'Cheerio, stranger.'

He jumped suddenly into the air and clicked his

heels like Charlie Chaplin. A couple of people turned and stared. Then he disappeared through the door of the newspaper office where he worked.

I went up to Boots and selected the toothpaste and shampoo Mum wanted. There was a mirror on the cosmetics counter and I stopped to look at my ears.

Then I went to the counter and paid. As the salesgirl handed me my bag of things, I saw Emma and Linda on the pavement outside. I must show them my earrings. I waved at them through the glass but they didn't see me.

'Your receipt's in the bag,' said the salesgirl.

I dashed from the counter to the door, just as Emma and her mum were about to pass outside. I jumped forward, making the door open, and as if by magic I appeared at their side.

'Hello. Hey! Do you know what's happened to me?'

Linda turned towards me. She had lost even more weight since I had last seen her. Her face was thin, and without any weight, her nose was bigger and sharper, while her mouth was tighter, smaller and rounder.

'I don't know how you have the cheek. You actually take my breath away, Phoebe. Do you know that?'

I'd heard Linda angry before, but never had I heard her talk in this cold, ferocious way.

'Come down here,' said Linda.

'Phoebe,' she continued, as we stepped along the

pavement. We stopped in front of the first window of Boots. The girl who had just served me was on the other side of the glass, perched on her stool.

'I want to let you know something so there's no possible misunderstanding. I respect you and your mother too much for this to go unsaid. I let you into my life. I opened my house to you. And what have you done in return for me, Phoebe, for me, who's never shown you a whit of harm? You've destroyed my life, that's all, destroyed it.

'Last Saturday three men came to the house and you knew – and don't try to pretend you didn't know, you're almost twelve years old, madam, catch yourself on – and you knew that you are not to let strangers into my house. But what did you do? You asked them in, you practically took them on a guided tour. They went away, these men you had invited into my house, and you probably thought nothing more about what had happened, and that's what ignorant little girls seem to have a great talent for doing, not thinking.

'Well, let me explain to you what that lack of thinking has brought about. The Army have said to Arthur he can't come to my house any more. The Army have said he can't see me any more. Not in my house, not in Enniskillen, not in Northern Ireland. If I want to see him I have to go to Scotland, or London. When you so blithely opened the door, that's what you let into my life. Thank you, Phoebe, thank you very, very much.'

'But I didn't let them in,' I said, 'or show them round. Emma told me to let them in.'

I looked at my friend. She had turned her face away and was staring across the road. All I saw was the side of her fringe, the curtain of hair that came down from her head and the nose, the sharp and pointed nose, just like her mother's nose, I realised.

'Don't, don't, Phoebe, don't insult me,' said Linda wearily. 'I know exactly what happened, I know exactly what you did.'

'No, you don't,' I wailed.

A woman passer-by turned and stared at us.

'No, you don't,' I repeated, more quietly.

'What you have done, Phoebe,' said Linda firmly, 'is to take something very precious, drop it on the floor, and smash it underfoot.'

'But I didn't!' I shouted. My face was reddening. I was a bag of tears and I was going to burst. 'I didn't do anything.'

'Don't talk to me about what you did and did not do, Phoebe. I'm living through this. I'll be the judge of that. You have destroyed my life, you vain, stupid, little girl. Come on, Emma.'

'But I didn't. I didn't.' She was talking as if I'd gone and asked the IRA to come and get Arthur. At the same time I heard myself saying the fatal words, 'I'm sorry,' before I was able to stop myself.

'Well, at least you have the good grace to admit you've done wrong. Oh, I'm sure you're sorry, I'm sure you're very sorry.'

Linda began to weep, big tears spilling from her bright eyes and rolling down her cheeks. My own tears came, hot and salty.

'Come on, Emma,' Linda muttered again.

I tried to move across the pavement in order to look at my friend but Linda got between us and pulled Emma away.

Then they were gone. I began to cry in earnest, and my throat hurt as it always does when I cry, and my thoughts were filled with hope after this last moment on the pavement. There was hope here. Emma was torn between Mother and friend, and so what else could she do in this situation except stare up the street and refuse to look me in the eye? Linda, of course, couldn't let me see my friend's face.

I heard knocking on glass. I looked and saw it was the Boots salesgirl. Her expression was troubled as she mouthed at me, 'Are you all right?'

I nodded frantically, and wiping my face on my cuff, I hurried down the street.

5 Bad to worse

I went to the door of the building where Dad worked. I stopped. I got out my hanky and I blew my nose and I wiped my face. I didn't want Dad to see a wet and tear-stained face. When he left me I was happy. That was the way I wanted him to see me again.

I opened the door and went over to the counter and asked if I could see my father.

'I'm afraid he went out, Miss Rodgers,' said the girl in the red uniform, 'just a few minutes ago. He had to go to Belleek. He won't be back until after lunch.'

I felt like sitting down, right there on the floor, and bursting into tears. How long since we'd said goodbye in the street? Five minutes? Ten minutes? How long was I in Boots? How long was Linda shouting at me in the street? It couldn't be more than fifteen minutes since we said goodbye.

'Would you like to sit down?' said the girl behind the counter. 'Are you all right? You look very white.'

I heard myself saying, 'No, I'm all right, no, don't worry,' as I glided back across the room and floated through the door.

What was I going to do? I had to ask myself this question as if I was talking to a child who wouldn't listen.

Well, I told myself, I must not cry. No, I definitely must not cry. Absolutely. I must stay calm. Absolutely. Was I to ring home? It was not ten o'clock. Mum wouldn't have left the house yet. The boys were probably still in their pyjamas. There was no point in ringing. I had to get through this by myself. I had to stand on my own two feet for once.

I looked the other way along the street. I couldn't believe my eyes. It was Emma. She was coming to make up. She was coming to tell me how awful her mother was. She was coming to tell me I was her friend.

Then I blinked. It wasn't Emma. It was a girl who looked and was dressed quite like her. I felt cheated. At the same time my heart was beating and my hands were hot. I needed to calm down.

Then, the idea hit me, the pool. That was the plan, so why didn't I just stick to it? Go down, swim in the cool, clear water; wash my hair afterwards in the hot, steaming showers; dry my hair in the hot air of the hair dryers, and comb it straight. When Mum collected me at eleven, I would be gleaming and clean and new.

Stepping down from the kerb and moving carefully across the empty road, I made a mental note to get some twenty pence pieces for the hair dryer at reception when I bought my ticket.

A few minutes later, I walked out of the changing room. The pool was quiet and almost empty. The slide which caused me to break my front tooth was gone. The only sign that it had once been there was a brown metal stain on the tiles at the side.

I clambered down the steps at the deep end and then fell back into the water. In my nose I felt the chlorine immediately. It was a sort of sore feeling.

I began to swim and, as I swam, I began to hear in my head what I wanted to say to Linda:

. . . It was your daughter who said to let them in, it wasn't me. Why aren't you angry with her? Because you have to have someone to blame and you've chosen me to be your scapegoat. Well, it's not true, and it's not fair. You've been horrid and wicked and vile and you hurt me when you shouted at me in the street and I never want to see you again. And don't think I'm not going to tell my mum. I'm going to tell her straight after swimming and I hope she stops being your friend . . .

I reached the shallow end, and as I reached forward for the gully in the wall – I was going to turn round, push with my feet against the tiles and swim another length – I saw my hand was shaking. This was rage, I realised. No, it was something more than rage. It was the biggest, biggest feeling that had ever happened to me. It felt like the moment in *Alice in Wonderland* when Alice swallows the contents of the bottle on the glass table, and grows so big she fills the entire room.

I couldn't swim on. I knew that. I got myself in front of a grille through which warm water comes into the pool. I let the hot water press on my body. It was not just my hand that was shaking. It was all of me. My heart was racing. I thought I heard my blood as it jumped through my veins. I decided to stay still and wait. With the bubbles pressing against me, I would feel better in a few minutes.

So, I stayed there in the shallow end with the water bubbling against me. After a few minutes, I no longer heard the shouts of the children splashing around me, or the quiet talk of the old women as they swam up and down. My mind went quite blank and as time trickled on I felt myself separating from what happened in the street outside Boots. It was like something was stuck to me and then very slowly the adhesive which attached this feeling came undone, and finally, it floated away from me like a balloon rising into the sky.

Then I heard the shrill blast of a whistle. I saw the life guard talking sternly to a boy in the water. I looked round at the clock. It was a quarter to eleven. I had hung there in the water for forty-five minutes, yet to me it seemed as though only a few seconds had passed. I realised I must hurry. I had to meet Mum outside at eleven.

I went to the changing room. I undressed. I scrubbed my head in the shower. I came out and I rubbed my skin with the towel until it burned. I dressed quickly. On the way out I passed the hair dryer. I had the money but I thought, why bother?

I walked along the corridor and across the foyer. The wet of my hair seeped through my dress but my hair would dry soon enough. It was summer, wasn't it? It would be tangled, of course, but I could comb it. Or not. Anyway, who cares, I thought.

I pushed open the door. The frame was aluminium and it squeaked. I walked out and it swung shut behind with another squeak. I was on a patio. There were flattened rounds of grey and white chewing gum all over the paving stones. In the flower bed, at the side, the earth was covered with bits of bark. These were brown and swollen with wet.

The car pulled up. Our car. Red, dull red. Mum at the wheel. The boys in the back.

Mum smiled as she lent across and opened the door on the front passenger side.

'Well, let's see,' she called, as I ducked my head and swung into the seat. 'Let's see. How was it? Did your dad stay with you?'

I closed the door and stared ahead.

'Well. Come on. Is something the matter?'

'No.'

I lifted my hair.

'Oh lovely,' said Mum, 'but now I don't want you to get any older, Phoebe. I want you to stop growing. Isn't that right, boys?'

'What?' said Fred.

'We don't want Phoebe to grow any more. Shall we take her to the hospital and get a pill to keep her just the way she is?'

I snorted.

'What is it, Phoebe?'

I didn't look at Mum but I knew by her tone she was squinting as she stared at me.

'Did something happen with Dad? You didn't have a row, did you?'

'No,' I said emphatically. 'I'm fine.' Then I added tentatively, 'Leave me alone.'

'My goodness me, almost twelve going on twenty-two,' exclaimed Mum. 'Can't take a joke.'

She released the hand brake. The car rolled forward.

When we got home I went straight upstairs and went and lay on my bed. I stared at the shelves with my glass animals. It was that special time of the day when the sun fell directly on them and the wall behind was a mixture of sunshine and colour. This only lasted a few minutes. Then the sun moved on and was gone.

'Phoebe,' I heard Mum shouting from below, 'Phoebe. Can you come downstairs?'

I had been waiting for the sun to shine like it was and now that it was happening, she was calling me down.

'What? What do you want?'

'Come down, would you, please.'

Behind the politeness there was testiness. Oh, mothers, mothers, mothers!

'Yes, yes, coming . . .'

I went out, walked sullenly across the landing and stomped down the stairs one step at a time.

Mum was in the hall at the bottom and she said, 'Come down, Phoebe, I want to talk to you about something.'

'What.'

'Phoebe! Just come down, will you?'

She went through the door and into Dad's study. Why did she want to talk to me in there?

'I've just had Dad on the phone.'

'Yes.'

'He said something rather odd happened. Apparently a girl from Boots popped into the newspaper office.'

Any interest I had in this conversation vanished, and in its place came a sour feeling. I knew what was coming. Well, I wasn't going to talk about it. And what was Mum going to do? Speak to Linda? That would just make a bad situation worse. It was pointless. The woman was deranged. The best thing was just to forget everything, just as I had managed to do for those forty-five minutes in the pool. Let time pass. Then, maybe, when I went back to school, Emma and I would say hello to one another and all this would be forgotten and we could get on with our lives.

'This salesgirl guessed you were Dad's daughter by your accent, and she knew Dad by sight, she'd seen him in the street. That's what living in a small town is all about. Everybody knows everybody else's business.

'Anyway, this woman asked for Dad and said she was rather concerned because she said she thought she saw someone speaking to you in the street and that you began to cry. She didn't know who they were. They had their back to the window.'

'That's rubbish,' I said, blankly. 'She must have mistaken me for someone else. I didn't talk to anyone.'

'Are you sure?'

'Yes.'

'Oh, come on, Phoebe, did you talk to anyone?'

'No.'

'Are you sure you're sure?'

'Of course I'm sure. I went to Boots and then I went to the swimming pool. And I didn't talk to anyone.'

'You're sure?'

'I know what I did. What are you checking up on me for? Don't you trust me?'

'Apparently you called into the office looking for Dad. One of the girls at the desk told him. She thought you looked distressed.'

'Oh yes. I'd wanted to get some money.'

'Money, I gave you money, I gave you plenty of money.'

'I tried to get change in Boots for the hair dryer at the pool, but they didn't have any. They never have any in the pool, so I thought, I'll call in on Dad and get some from him.'

'Really?'

She looked at me with her I-really-don't-believe-a-word-you're-saying face.

'Really,' I said brazenly and nodded. 'I wish you wouldn't check up on me all the time. You treat me like a baby.'

My voice trembled. I wanted to cry and weep and shout out everything that had happened. But Mum thought the emotion in my voice was because I was upset with her. I was using one set of feelings to make her believe what wasn't true. I saw this with the bit of me that's above and looks down. I also saw this was a brilliant performance. If I quivered my lip and stamped my foot and let my eyes fill with tears, she would believe what I was saying.

'You're always checking on me,' I began, 'because you don't trust me, and because you think I'm like Fred and Tom, and any minute I might wander off and drown in the lake, when all along I'll just be asleep in my bedroom. You said it this morning; you said you wanted to give me a pill to stop me growing; well, you can't stop me growing, I am growing, and I want you to leave me alone.'

I burst into tears as I fled from the study. My throat ached as I ran up the stairs, two at a time, and the walls and the banister rail were a blur through my salty tears.

I got into my bedroom and slammed the door behind with all my might. It pleased me to feel the force of the door under my feet as it travelled along the floorboards. I looked at my animals but the sun had passed on and the lovely coloured blobs of light dancing on the wall were gone. Mum had cheated me out of my one pleasure that day when she made me go downstairs. I threw myself on to my bed and sobbed loudly into the pillow.

6 Frozen out at Rossnowlagh

We turned off the Ballyshannon road and nosed down the hill. The lane twisted and turned like a piece of string. Then we came round a corner and I saw Rossnowlagh below. I saw row after row after row of mobile homes, the beach covered with tiny cars and tinier people, and finally, in the distance, I saw the sea. As we dropped down and the world rushed up to meet us, I thought it was like being on a plane and flying in to an airport.

We landed and taxied along the road that follows the sea. I remembered driving around this same corner when I was with John and his parents. I didn't like this, but I realised it was inevitable I was going to remember what happened then.

Definitely, I thought, I shouldn't have let Mum persuade me to come and spend the night in Jude's mobile. I should not have listened when she said it would cheer me up. I should have stayed with Dad and gone to the concert in Belfast.

What? I thought, and had two hours of Dvorak and his New World symphony? I'd have been bored out of my mind. What was I thinking?

I decided I must not think about *any of this any more*. So I made a deliberate decision to turn and look out of the window. I saw cows with long horns in a field, sand dunes with long, spiky grass growing all over them, and then the entrance of Jude's site appeared.

We turned in and bumped over the ground to the end of the site that was closest to the sea. We stopped at Jude's mobile and got out.

It was a long, green oblong building, with vast, oblong picture windows. Inside I saw a purple settee and purple walls. Jude was at the kitchen sink. She saw us, waved and rushed out. She wore a hippie tie-dye dress and big parrot earrings. Her face was red and round with a small mouth and two prominent front teeth which sat on her lower lip. She and Mum had recently become friends – they went to the same yoga class.

'Welcome,' said Jude, tickling me under the chin. For some reason she had it in her head that I was really five years old rather than almost twelve.

Yes, perhaps the concert would have been better, after all.

'Come on,' I said to my two brothers.

We were in the main room in Jude's mobile and we

were all in our swimming costumes. 'I'll take you down to the sea,' I said, 'but I warn you, you go out too far and you drown, that's your own look-out, all right?'

'Phoebe!' said Mum, and gave me one of her looks. 'Try and be a little kinder, will you?'

'All right, Mum, you tell them. They have to do what I say. I tell them to come back out of the water, then they come out and no mucking about.'

'You hear that, boys,' Mum shouted after Fred and Tom as they rushed towards the door. 'You do what Phoebe tells you.'

'Yeah, yeah,' they shouted, and the door banged after them.

'Oh well, better get going,' I said.

I picked up the towels and went out after Fred and Tom.

The day outside was warm and fine. There was a breeze and the sun was shining. I walked across the grass. I saw my skinny brothers ducking through the gate ahead.

'Boys, mind the cars.'

'Yeah, Phoebe,' they shouted back.

So they heard me. That was something.

A few seconds later I went through the gate myself. It closed after me. There was a spring which did this automatically and the spring squeaked.

I followed the path down the side of a dune. The

soft sand under my feet was hard to walk on because it kept giving way.

At the end I stepped off the path and I was on the beach. There were stones lying in the sand here and a life belt tied on to a white cross. There was a girl's swimsuit hanging from the cross.

I walked on through the parked cars and the picnic tables, the wind breaks and the day trippers lying on towels. I saw my brothers sprinting towards the sea. I heard the sea break on the shore and I saw the line of foam made by the wave. A gull screeched and I remembered John's dolphin and the way I had torn it off. I felt a stab in me. Why had I done that? He'd only pushed me over. It wasn't that big a deal. But that's what I'd done. And once I'd given it to him, what else could he do but throw it away? His behaviour was childish, of course, but now I saw it was absolutely predictable.

I left the towels down on dry sand and walked on.

Yes, I was stupid. Very stupid. If only we were still friends, John and me. I'd have someone to talk to about all the horrible things that had happened. Someone who wasn't a grown-up.

I came to the edge of the sea where the sand was wet and hard. The water lapped over my feet and I gasped with the cold. My brothers were already up to their waists. They were jumping up and down and splashing water over one another. They were howling with the joy of being in the sea and the cold of the water at the same time. They never seemed to feel the temperature, I noticed. Whereas me, I've always felt the cold. As Mum says, I'm really a Mediterranean baby.

I felt another stab. How I wished Sylvia hadn't got ill. Or that I had somebody else to talk to. Anybody. I hated being with myself and these terrible thoughts that were churning round and round in my head.

I went out another step and gasped again.

Then the quite unexpected idea crossed my mind that I might bump into Emma or even Linda here. I looked along the beach. It stretched into the distance for miles and miles. It was very unlikely, I told myself, very unlikely. At the same time, my heart was banging. I really did not want to see either of them.

Now I was angry with myself. Why had I let Mum persuade me to come? Oh, I was such a blithering idiot. As usual, I had just gone along with what was happening, and now I was going to reap the consequences.

I walked on, the sea rising as I went.

'I'm going out to swim,' I called to my brothers as I passed them.

When the level of the water was up to my waist, I let myself fall head first into the freezing Atlantic.

Half an hour later, I followed Fred and Tom out of the water. As I waded after them towards the shore, I felt the warmth of the air on my body.

They screeched in the way that little boys screech, and dashed across the sand towards our towels. I glanced sideways at the mountains to the north. They were deep green, with a blue sky above them filled with great white clouds. My skin tingled. I felt awake. Alive. Because of the cold and the movement of the water, I thought, I had left misery behind and now I was happy.

So what is it about me? Even though I know what will help when I'm in a mood, I still can't help myself. The help has to come from outside.

Why was that?

It didn't seem fair. Or right. I thought there was a reason for everything in the world, even bad things like famine and disease.

These thoughts took about a second.

Then I saw this great sand-castle. There were five great towers joined by thick walls with battlements and a moat. Two boys and their dad had made it. To get water from the sea to the castle, they were digging a trench. There was only a foot left to dig. I stopped and watched them lift away the sand with their plastic spades. Then they were finished and the foamy ocean swept along the trench and filled the moat.

'Hey!' I said.

It was impressive. I walked on and glanced ahead. Where were Fred and Tom? On a beach if I'm walking towards someone I have to keep looking at them otherwise I might lose sight of them.

Oh yes, there they were. They were talking to somebody. A girl. Who? She wore a black swimming costume. Then I saw the hair and the shape of the nose. Oh no! It was Em.

So Em was here, as I'd feared, and no doubt her mother was here as well.

Then Emma looked up. She saw that I had seen. She ruffled Fred's hair and he ducked away from her. He was laughing. She walked away.

I watched her move off along the beach. I watched her until she was lost in the crowds and I couldn't see her anymore. She didn't want to see me but did I want to see her?

I walked up to my brothers, found a towel and began to dry myself.

'I don't understand it,' said Mum.

She was standing at the sink washing the dinner plates. Jude's mobile smelt of fish. We'd had grilled mackerel for supper and the door was propped open with the broom to let the air circulate.

'I saw Linda,' Mum continued, 'and I said, "Hello,"

and she looked at me as if I didn't exist and walked right on.'

I wiped the brown Formica table. I gathered the fish bones and fish skin and drops of tomato ketchup into a heap, then I lifted the bin up to the edge of the table and swept everything in.

'From one day to the next we've gone from friends, good friends, close friends, to being not enemies but strangers.'

'I'm going to the beach,' I said.

'Oh.' Mum looked at me. She seemed not to have noticed that I might have heard what she had said. She scratched the side of her nose with her wrist. Her hand was covered with a white glove of soap suds.

'I'm just going to have a little walk,' I explained.

'Yes, you do that, love, walk off the dinner,' said Jude. 'If I had any discipline, I'd join you.'

Jude drained her wine glass and wiped her mouth.

I felt strange, and sort of annoyed with her.

'It's not bad this stuff in a box, is it? I don't need another glass,' said Jude, as the drink bubbled and spattered in her glass. 'This is pure greed.'

'Go ahead, treat yourself,' said Mum. She scrubbed a plate and set it on the rack at the side.

'No later than eight, Phoebe,' Mum continued, and looked at me.

'All right,' I said.

I hurried from the door and down the steps. I wanted to get away from the smell of the fish. I wanted to get away from the small confined space inside the mobile. I wanted to get away from Jude. She had had more wine than was good for her and she was woozy and I've never liked adults when they go soft and limp with drink. It's disgusting.

I wanted to be alone on the beach. I wanted freedom, space, sky.

At least this is what I told myself.

I went through the gate and down the path of soft sand to the beach.

I was going to walk along to the rocks at the far end. I was going to scavenge for razor shells and strange pieces of wood. Once I had found a wooden box filled with tea among these rocks. The tea was ruined by the salt water but the box was fine. It had Dimbula Estate Broken Orange Pekoe written on the sliding lid. We had the box at home and Dad kept his small chess pieces in it. Perhaps I would find something else as good as that. That's why I'd come out. That's what I told myself.

I cut across the sand and reached the edge of the sea. The beach was quite empty except for one or two people strolling like myself. I saw a black Labrador chasing into the sea after a stick.

After walking for a while I looked up. At this point

on the beach there was a little valley that ran back into the dunes. You could only see into this valley when you got to this spot. I could see into it now. I saw there was a fire burning. Grey smoke trailed up into the air. There were some girls sitting around the fire.

I had known I would find this, hadn't I?

From the moment I left Jude's mobile. No, from before I'd left Jude's mobile.

I'd seen Em in the afternoon and it didn't take much brains to work out that I would find Nicola and Sarah as well.

And now I had. For there they were, sitting round the fire with Em. Linda was nowhere to be seen. There were my friends. There was the gang. They were there in the dunes, and I was by the sea.

And now I had found what I hoped and what I expected to find, did I have the courage to do what I had told myself, what I had promised myself I should do if I found them, as I had expected?

Oh yes, there was no way out now. I had to walk over.

I turned my back on the sea and began to walk across the beach. A crisp packet blew across my path. Smoky bacon. I looked ahead. My friends were clustered around the fire, evenly spaced. They were all looking at the flames. They hadn't seen me. At least they hadn't looked up as if they had seen me. Not yet. And no one had pointed either. Not yet. But they must have seen me, I thought, they must have.

I walked steadily forward but the fire and my friends remained the same size they were when I'd seen them from the shore. Or they appeared to remain the same size. Then, suddenly, they were bigger and I was closer. Much. I saw what they were wearing and I saw they were holding sticks in the fire. They were roasting marshmallows, I guessed. That's why they were all looking at the flames. If I shouted they would hear me. But I wasn't going to shout. I'd already decided against that. In fact, I'd decided everything I was now doing in the moments before I told Mum I was going out for a walk. I was going to walk up to them, and I was going to say, 'Hello.'

This was the plan. But now I had found them, I saw that my plan was a dream.

They weren't shouting or walking or pushing one another towards the sea, which was what I'd imagined I'd find them doing.

No. My three friends were clustered round the fire. They were quiet. The flames were flickering on their faces. Each held a stick and on the end of each stick there was white or pink goo. Now someone laughed. That was Nicola. She began to chew her marshmallow. The hot sweet stretched like nougat and then a thick strand dribbled down her chin. The others laughed. I was close. Close enough to hear. Close enough to see the bag of marshmallows on the ground. I saw Nicola take out another, spear it and put it in the fire. Why had they kept their backs towards me. Surely I was so close to them now they must have realised that I was here? They must have. Yet they were acting as if I wasn't there.

There was laughter again as Em chewed at her marshmallow and a long pink length fell down her front.

They must know I'm here. They couldn't not see me. Surely, surely they had to see me? I was only half a dozen paces away. But no. They didn't see. They were refusing to see me. It really was as if I was invisible. If I walked up and sat down, I realised, no one was going to speak to me. If I found a piece of sharp wood and asked for the packet of marshmallows, no one was going to hand them to me. If I chewed on a hot marshmallow and the hot, gooey centre dropped on to my lap, no one was going to laugh.

I saw this future as clearly as I saw them at this moment. I saw that I didn't exist. That's what had happened. I had disappeared, as if by magic. I also saw that I should not have come to find them. I should have been able to predict this. Should have. Should have.

There was only one way now to go. I had to turn

round. But not right round. I wasn't going to head back to the site with my tail between my legs. Oh no. That would have given Em complete triumph.

No. I was going to walk to the end and comb the beach like I planned. They would see I didn't run back to Mum. They would see I kept going.

As it turned out, this little victory was denied me. I walked away. I got down to the rocks. I looked for shells and bits of wood, but my heart wasn't really in it. That's an understatement. My heart wasn't in it at all. I wanted to run back to the fire and shout, '*What* is this? *What* on earth's going on?'

After about twenty minutes I turned round and walked back along the beach towards Jude's. When I reached the spot where you can see the little valley in the dunes, I turned to see if my friends were there. The fire was there, all right, I saw it burning away, a column of smoke rising into the air, but Em and the gang were gone.

An hour or more had passed since I last stood here, and night was coming on. The sand dunes were no longer a series of rolling shapes which connected together, but a long dark form like some huge sleeping monster. The clouds overhead had changed colour from white to purple and pink, while the sky behind them had darkened from blue to plum.

I walked across the sand and stopped at the fire.

There were a couple of big pieces of wood burning away fiercely and I supposed these were put on quite some time ago. I looked around and saw their sticks with bits of marshmallow stuck to them. I saw the flattened sand where my friends had sat. Then I saw there were words written in the sand in front of the fire.

I got close and peered down. The light was fading but I had no trouble reading them.

Phoebe, I read, *Go away*.

7 A bad dream

I took the glass animal down from the shelf in my bedroom. It was a performing seal with a ball on its nose. There was a red blob inside the ball and a blue blob inside the seal.

I dropped this glass animal into the metal waste-paper bin on the floor. I heard the glass shattering. I peered into the bin.

The tail had broken off one end of the body and the head had broken off the other end of the body. Funnily enough, the ball was still attached to the nose of the seal.

It did not come as a surprise, what I saw. Except now I saw the three pieces in the bottom of the bin, my eyes filled with tears and the back of my throat pained.

I wanted the animal broken. I wanted all the animals broken. I wanted all the animals off the shelves and cleared away. They were a stupid, ridiculous collection of objects. They belonged to childhood. Which was over. Gone. Finished. The whole lot needed clearing out and throwing away.

I was determined to go ahead. I was determined to go forward. I knew that in order to grow up, I had to do this. But for all my determination now, as I looked into the bin, I was crying. I didn't want to do this.

But you must, said a voice from another part of myself.

Did I have the strength to reach up to the shelf and take the next piece? It was a Scottish terrier with pointed green ears and a green tail.

I must destroy it, I thought. My twelfth birthday was coming any day. I didn't need these girlie things.

But I loved the little terrier.

I had to, I told myself. I snatched it down and threw it into the bucket.

Instead of just breaking into separate pieces like the seal, this piece shattered into many, many pieces, tiny pieces. I felt a sort of happiness but also a sort of wrench inside. I loved my dog. I wanted my dog gone. I wanted my dog destroyed. I was glad it was gone. I was happy. It was childish.

I peered into the bottom of the bin. Tiny bits of glass all over the bottom. They shone like diamonds. All that remained of the original was a single green-tipped ear. Ha! Good riddance. Excellent.

Time to get going, time to clear everything out, and not a second too soon.

I lifted up the bin and got my hand underneath the

base. I remembered the waiters in Italy carried the ice buckets in exactly the same way.

I ran my other hand along the shelf and everything tumbled forward towards the rim. The elephant and the two baby elephants. The anteater with the long tongue and the tiny little fly on the end of the long tongue. The two giraffes with black spots. The camel with two humps and a tiny real leather saddle. The donkey hitched to the strange cart with wooden wheels which I bought in Rossnowlagh, as it happened. The lion on the box shaking his mane . . .

At first, as one piece after another hit the bottom of the bin, the sound of breakage was distinct. The noise of the elephant breaking was different from the noise of the two baby elephants breaking. But when I reached the end of the first shelf everything was overlapping and the noise of the donkey smashing and the lion smashing were mixed together.

I moved my hand up to the next shelf and swept it along as fast as I was able. I felt exhilarated and happy. I believed that if I kept up the speed of destruction I would reach a point of joy where nothing could touch me. No matter what went wrong, no matter what happened or did not happen in the future between Em and me, I wouldn't care.

To reach this state I had to go faster and harder. I positively whipped my arm along the third shelf. The animals didn't so much tumble one after the other, as fly in a group towards the mouth of the bin, crash into the bottom a fraction of a second later and smash into smithereens.

I paused, breathless. I must keep going. Faster and faster. Whatever else, I must keep going. I must not think.

I dragged the chair over from the table and jumped up on it. I threw my arm along the fourth shelf. The animals flew into the air, seemed to hover there for an instant like a cloud, and then clattered into the bin. I swept my hand along the fifth shelf. The noise of breaking glass was continuous. I reached up to the sixth and last shelf and again I swept my hand along it in a single fierce movement. Together they fell. The frog with the blue eyes sitting on the glass water lily. The mare and foal. The whale with water shooting from his spout. The budgie in the cage with the thinnest glass bars. And finally, the robin with the berry in his mouth. He hit the edge of the bin and broke in half. The two pieces spun into the air. I held out the bin and caught them one after the other. I heard the pieces as they hit the bottom of the bin.

Then there was silence. It was over. I had done it. I had cleared out my shelves. I had thrown out my childhood. I felt a strange sense of excitement. I looked into the bin. Lying piled in the bottom, I saw lots of pieces of glass, some with bits of colour in them, but for the most part they were clear, transparent.

Now that I had cleared everything away, what I expected to feel was pure joy, happiness.

Yet now as I stared, now, over the rim and into the bottom of the bin, I felt awful.

My legs trembled. I jumped down from the chair.

How could I? I loved that robin redbreast. I saved up two weeks' pocket money to buy the donkey and cart. The camel came from Egypt. Sylvia's dad had brought it back for me.

My eyes filled with tears. I had made a most terrible mistake. I dropped the bin on the ground. The sun shone through my window and fell on the empty shelves. I saw the white light of the sun, the yellow grain of the wooden shelves. Why had I done this? What possessed me?

I opened my mouth. I wanted to howl. This howl was going to raise the roof off the house.

But I never got it out. Because instead of the noise coming out of my mouth, I opened my eyes.

I was not at home. So where was I?

Then, into my thoughts, rushed the memory of what I had just done. Surely, I thought, surely I hadn't smashed all those beautiful glass animals? Of course, I hadn't, had I? I'd had a nightmare and in the nightmare that's what I did. But in real life the glass animals were safe.

I wanted to look at them suddenly. I wanted to see them. I wanted to touch them. I wanted to feel their cold, shiny hard surfaces. But I couldn't because I was not at home. I was in Jude's mobile. I was at Rossnowlagh.

The dining-room table turned into a double bed and that's where I was. It was a small double bed. Tom was jammed on one side of me and Fred on the other. I heard the slow in and out of their breathing. I felt their bodies against me. There was a very faint smell of the mackerel we'd had for dinner hanging in the air. My cheeks were puffy and wet. The tears were flowing hard and fast. There was a pain in the back of my throat. I felt miserable and wretched. It was only a dream but the dream had made me feel as bad as if I really had smashed everything up.

'Phoebe, is that you?' I heard Mum call. She was in a sleeping bag on the sofa under the picture window at the front of the mobile. It overlooked the sea.

I licked the tears from round my mouth and swallowed.

'Yes.'

'You're crying,' said Mum.

'Yes.'

'Why are you crying?'

Why was I crying?

'I don't know,' I said.

239

Of course I did. Yet how did I explain to her? I had a friend and her mother had shouted at me in the street and now I had lost that friend and my other friends along with her.

'I had a bad dream,' I said.

'Come over, Phoebe. Come over here. Come on.'

I slid down the bed and slipped under the bottom of the duvet. When I put my feet on the floor I felt the linoleum was cold and I gasped a little. I wiped the arm of my nightdress over my face and my nose and my mouth. The sleeve went wet.

'Come on, Phoebe,' Mum called and I saw her sit up. She unzipped the sleeping bag. Then she pulled the bottom of the bag from under her and threw it over herself like a duvet.

'Come on. Don't stand there shivering. I'll make you nice and warm.'

She was going to ask me what the matter was. What was I going to say? I saw a message in the sand that read, *Phoebe, Go away.*

I lifted my foot from the floor and the skin of my sole made a noise like escaping air. How did I tell her? And did I dare? Would she tell me I was being silly? Would she tell me not to worry? Would she tell me I was making a mountain out of a mole hill?

I took another step and again my skin made a noise as it came away.

'Come on,' she called, 'don't dilly-dally.'

Don't dilly-dally. That's how she spoke to Fred and Tom. She hadn't spoken to me like that in ages. Dilly-dally. Where did that word come from?

I took another step and another step and another step.

Her arm came up and took my hand. She pulled. I let myself be tugged down. Now I was beside her on the couch. She turned to face me. At the same time she threw the sleeping bag around me to cover my back. Great sobs ran through me. My cheeks were sodden. I was not able to see. There were even tears in my mouth. I could taste their salt.

Mum folded her arms around me and pulled me closer. My head was on the pillow. I smelt Mum's hair. It smelt of shampoo. The pillow also smelt faintly – of detergent, I thought. Mum's nightdress smelt too, of perfume. She often wore perfume at night. She said she liked to go to sleep with the smell of something beautiful around her. I think she wore the perfume for Dad.

'Darling,' she whispered. Her hand was on my face. Her dry palm skimmed over a wet cheek.

'I had a nightmare,' I said, 'I dreamt I smashed all my glass animals.'

How are you going to tell her? I wondered as I said this. I had a friend until her mother blamed me for something I did not do, and now I'd lost that friend.

241

'I saw Linda tonight,' said Mum.

My heart froze. I let out another sob.

'After you went out, I walked down to the shop,' she began. Her voice was gentle. 'I had to buy some things for Jude. I had just paid and I was moving towards the door when Linda drove up and jumped out of her car. She came in at the very same moment as I was leaving, so it was impossible to avoid one another.

'I said, "Hi, Linda," and she looked at me with the most dreadful expression. I said, "Is something the matter?" She said nothing, not a word. She just looked straight at me. It wasn't an angry look but it wasn't a friendly one either.

'I had the impression she wished I wasn't there, she wished she could make me vanish into thin air and disappear out of her life forever.

'I said, "Have I done something to offend you?" because that's what I felt she felt. She told me, "No," just like that. Then she walked past me and went into the shop. It was as if we'd never been friends, as if she'd never spent the night in the house, never drunk Dad's whiskey. It was as if I no longer existed. For some reason, which as yet I didn't understand, she'd snapped her fingers and made me invisible.

'I was puzzled and I was upset but also I've known something's been wrong since she came to the house when there were all those dramas about Arthur. I'd spoken to her on the phone a couple of times since then, and on both occasions she was cold and off-hand. She didn't want to talk. So coming on top of those things, this business outside the shop didn't seem quite so strange.

'I walked back to the mobile. I put the boys to bed. Then we sat down together. It was quiet. You weren't back. I thought, I'll talk to Jude because she's friendly with Linda.

'I told Jude what had happened and Jude smiled and said yes, she wasn't surprised. She said that was Linda. She would blow hot and then she would blow cold. For two years, Jude explained, Linda didn't speak to her because of some trivial incident over a bill which Jude couldn't even remember now.

'So I said to Jude, "That's what's happened. I've done something to offend her." "Well, not you," said Jude, "It's Phoebe." "What?" I said. She said it again, "It's Phoebe." From what she'd gathered talking to Linda over the last couple of days, Arthur's been warned off her and Linda blames you, Phoebe. This was out of the blue and yet, after that weird visit we had last week, it made perfect sense. Of course it's also ridiculous. This thing with Arthur had nothing to do with you. But according to Jude, Linda's convinced herself that if you hadn't opened the door and let those men in, none of this would have happened, and Linda's one of these people who has to blame someone.'

'But I didn't let them in,' I said. 'Emma told me to open the door. Emma said to the one who wanted to come in, "Come in." I'd never have told him to come in. It wasn't my house.'

'Of course you wouldn't.' Mum's arms squeezed around my shoulders. 'Can I ask a question?' she said. 'You don't have to answer.'

The pillow was wet under my cheek. My hair was wet. The tears were in my ears. They were even on my sleepers from where they dripped on to my neck.

'Yes,' I said. My voice was muffled.

'Did Linda say something to you in town?'

I let out a great sob and nodded my head in the darkness.

'Did you see Emma today?'

I nodded my head again.

'And tonight?'

My head bobbed for the third time.

'When you got back from your walk,' said Mum, 'you were as white as a sheet. I guessed something awful had happened and it involved Emma. Don't tell me the details, just say if I'm vaguely right.'

'All right,' I agreed.

'She doesn't want to be your friend? That's what happened?'

Mum had guessed. She could still see inside my head, after all. 'Yes,' I said.

'Emma's probably too in awe of her mother, and too frightened of her mother to stand up for you. But I'm sure she knows what she's doing is wrong. I'm sure she knows it's cowardly not to stand up for you. She's not a bad kid.'

There was a piece of glass in my heart, but when Mum spoke it flew backwards out of my heart and vanished into the darkness.

'Will I see Dad tomorrow?' I asked.

'Of course you'll see Dad tomorrow. We'll go home tomorrow.'

'I'm sorry I'm not nicer to Fred and Tom,' I said.

Why this popped out at this moment, I've no idea. It just did.

'Don't worry,' said Mum. 'Don't you worry about that. You're good and kind and loyal. They love you. You mustn't worry.'

'How did you know what happened?' I whispered.

'Oh,' she whispered, 'I had nothing definite to go on, but there was one little thing after another and I worked it out.'

The sobs stopped. I rubbed my face against her nightdress and dried my eyes.

I told her that I loved her. She told me that she loved me.

Then we lay still, neither awake nor asleep, but in between. Outside the sky slowly turned from black to blue and the stars went out like lights. We sat on the sofa and with our noses against the window we watched the sun rise out of the sea and climb slowly into the heavens.

Postscript

At the end of the summer I went down the lane in my new uniform, and when I got to the end there was the pole on the other side of the road, the one I'd hit three times in a row with a stone. Some things might be different but some things never change. When I walked through the front door of my new school forty minutes later, who did I see before I saw anyone else? Emma, of course. And who was she talking to? Nicola and Sarah.

They were together again at break and I went up to them and I said, 'Hello,' and they said, 'Hello,' back. We had a strained conversation about the summer and we all complained about brothers and sisters and mothers and fathers. What happened on the beach was never mentioned. We all became friends of sorts again, but we were not as close as we had been before, and in time we made other friends. I saw John again as well in the weeks that followed the start of term. We were on the same bus, so sometimes we sat and talked. But we never talked about the necklace or what happened either.

At Christmas Linda called at our house with a tree. She had a new man, a forester, and he had given her two, she explained, and so she was giving us the spare rather than see it go to waste. She and Mum started to see each other once again, but they were not nearly as friendly as they were before. What happened was never discussed, but they both knew it was there and that it kept them apart.

Some say that it's better to get things out in the open but I don't know. Sometimes I think it's better not to.

Linda's never mentioned shouting at me in the street, nor has Emma ever talked about what happened, and I'm grateful in one sense, because if either of them did, that would bring it all up again and then we would have to go over everything. I don't want to do that because if they came out with the truth I would have to come out with the truth, my truth; and I don't think they'd like that. Because of what happened I found something out. I saw something about mother and daughter. I did not like what I saw but I think it may have made me wiser.

With the passing of time I see what has happened as like a fall in childhood. There was a lot of blood, a lot of pain, but then I got over it.

And they do say broken legs heal stronger.

Only *after* you are tempered, do you thank the hammer and the anvil.

Ulster Proverb